"Well, it's late,"
"I'd better get you h

He took one giant step back. *Kiss her?* he argued internally. *How can I kiss her? This isn't even supposed to be a date.*

"Right," she answered in a hushed tone. "I have to work tomorrow."

"Me, too."

His legs trembled slightly as he escorted Elizabeth to the truck, a passionate tension wafting in the air between them. The debate over whether he should have kissed her raged on in his mind.

At the Lamberts' door, he grasped her hand and shook it good night. "I had a great time. You're a fun pizza partner."

She stepped toward him. "I had a great time, too."

The moment lingered, and Kavan could feel a light sweat beading on his forehead. "Good night, Elizabeth."

He stepped back so quickly, he stumbled down the front porch steps.

"Kavan!"

"I'm all right, I'm all right," he shouted, getting his balance and hustling to his truck.

"Are you sure?" she called.

The melodious sound of her voice lingered in his ears as he headed toward home.

LYNN A. COLEMAN was raised on Martha's Vineyard and now calls Miami, Florida, home. She has three grown children and eight grandchildren. She is a minister's wife who writes to the Lord's glory. She serves as advisor of the American Christian Romance Writers. Lynn enjoys hearing from her readers; visit her Web page at: www.lynncoleman.com

RACHEL HAUCK lives in Palm Bay, Florida, with her husband Tony, a youth pastor. A graduate of Ohio State University with a degree in journalism, she is employed by a software company. She has worked for more than fifteen years with Tony in youth ministry where they focus on leadership training and whole-hearted devotion to Jesus. She is a worship leader and speaker. Rachel serves the writing community as the vice president of American Christian Romance Writers.

Books by Lynn A. Coleman

HEARTSONG PRESENTS
HP314—Sea Escape
HP396—A Time to Embrace
HP425—Mustering Courage
HP443—Lizzy's Hope
HP451—Southern Treasures
HP471—One Man's Honor
HP506—Cords of Love
HP523—Raining Fire

Don't miss out on any of our super romances. Write to us at the following address for information on our newest releases and club information.

Heartsong Presents Readers' Service
PO Box 721
Uhrichsville, OH 44683

Lambert's Pride

Lynn A. Coleman and Rachel Hauck

Heartsong Presents

From Lynn:
To my granddaughter Kayla and the love she's brought to our lives and who has a bit of Elizabeth Lambert inside of her.

From Rachel:
Thanks to Lynn for calling me one July afternoon with an invitation and an idea. Thanks to my husband Tony, ACRWCrit7, and my fireman brother Pete for his contribution and advice. And to Dad and Mom who always said I could.
    Dedicated to Jesus, my Beloved and my Friend.

A note from the Authors:
We love to hear from our readers! You may correspond with us by writing:

Lynn A. Coleman and Rachel Hauck
Author Relations
PO Box 719
Uhrichsville, OH 44683

ISBN 1-59310-077-9

LAMBERT'S PRIDE

Our mission is to publish and distribute inspirational products offering exceptional value and biblical encouragement to the masses.

PRINTED IN THE U.S.A.

one

Elizabeth Lambert rushed through the kitchen door and hustled up the back stairs to her room, taking them two at a time.

"Dinner's on the table, Beth," her grandma said when she scurried past.

"No time," Elizabeth called over her shoulder. "Sinclair's wants me to come in as soon as I can."

In her room, she shoved the door partially closed and slipped from the slacks and blouse she'd worn to Lambert's Furniture into her uniform for Sinclair's, the department store where she worked several evenings a week.

From the bottom of the stairs, Grandma admonished her, "You can't work seventy hours a week without taking time to eat a healthy meal."

"I'll get a burger on the way," Elizabeth replied in a clear, loud voice.

With quick, short strokes, she ran a comb through her hair and pulled it back with a red ribbon. A subtle knock caused her to turn toward the door. "Enter," she said.

Grandma pushed the door open and stood in the doorway, her hands on her ample hips. "A fast-food burger is not a healthy meal."

Elizabeth laughed and started to hang up the clothes she'd worn to the office. "I'm used to it."

Grandma settled on the edge of the bed. "Why don't you take a break from all this work? There's no need—"

"You know I didn't want to come to White Birch in the first place," Elizabeth interrupted, tossing her low-heeled pumps onto the closet floor in exchange for a pair of white sneakers. "But if Dad insists I take a break from school to learn the value of money and good, hard work, then *work* is what I'm going to do."

She plopped onto the floor and stuffed her feet into her white leather sneakers. "Besides, I've been living at this pace since my freshman year at college. Grabbing a burger on the run is nothing new."

"Doesn't mean I have to like it."

Elizabeth looked at her grandmother's wise, gentle face. "I appreciate your concern, but right now, eating a well-balanced meal is the least of my concerns."

Grandma stood and smiled. "You better run along, or you'll be late."

Elizabeth hopped up, then grabbed her backpack and car keys. In a soft tone, she admitted, "I know I don't seem grateful, Grandma, but I do appreciate all you and Grandpa have done for me."

"We know life in White Birch is a far cry from the life you can live in Boston, but we love having you here."

Elizabeth leaned over and kissed her grandma on the cheek. "Well, if I have to be someplace other than Boston, being with you and Grandpa is a pretty cool alternative."

Grandma beamed. "Well, hurry, or you won't even have time for a quick burger." She made a shuffling motion with her arms and feet.

Elizabeth chuckled and darted down the stairs with a quick glance at the large hall clock. She would barely make it on time even if she *didn't* stop for a burger.

Her father's classic 1973 Volkswagen Super Beetle sat on the edge of the driveway; its candy apple red paint glistened in the evening light. Tossing her backpack into the passenger seat, Elizabeth slipped in behind the wheel.

The restored car, a graduation present from her parents, came with a condition: Spend a season working in the family business in White Birch, New Hampshire. When she balked at the idea, they sweetened the deal, offering to pay all of her graduate school tuition if she agreed to their proposal.

Shifting into fourth gear, Elizabeth zipped through the center of White Birch. The quaint New England town looked to her as though it'd grown from a Norman Rockwell painting.

Remembering the discussion with her parents set her on edge. After all, at twenty-three, she had the right to make her own decisions about life. But in the whole vast scheme of things, she decided a summer in the quaint town was a small price to pay for an all-expense-paid ride to grad school—plus the title to the red classic car. She'd wanted to go to grad school for about as long as she wanted to inherit her father's vintage car.

To her surprise, Elizabeth enjoyed the few weeks she'd spent living with her grandparents, though their devotion to the Lord exposed her unrequited faith. The senior Lamberts sought God at every turn, over every issue. Even the decision to let Elizabeth live with them came after several days of prayer.

How could anyone depend on God so much? Elizabeth preferred to chart her own course in life, depending on reason instead of the ethereal world of prayer.

All at once, a loud bang resonated in her ears and the little car swerved hard to the right. Elizabeth gripped the steering wheel tighter, and with one foot on the brake and the other on the clutch, she slowed the car and forced it safely to the shoulder.

Trembling, she got out of the car and examined the outside. "Great," she mumbled, the flat right tire testifying to her problems. She knelt to inspect the damage. Pieces of shredded tire littered the road.

I'm going to be really late. She sighed, making her way to the front of the car. She popped the VW's round trunk and peered inside. *Figures. No spare.* She let the trunk close with a bang.

Propping herself against the trunk lid, Elizabeth contemplated her next move. She had her cell phone in her backpack, so she knew she could call one of her cousins for help. But calling on a Lambert meant the whole family would somehow become involved in this minor incident. During her short time in White Birch, Elizabeth had quickly learned that nothing seemed sacred or private among the Lambert clan.

I'll handle the problem myself. She stepped around to the passenger side, fetched her backpack, locked the doors, and started jogging toward Sinclair's.

❧

Kavan Donovan focused his binoculars and scanned a local camping area from the top of the run-down White Birch fire tower.

Aerial surveillance replaced most of the forest ranger's manual chores, but Kavan still climbed the tower to survey the area. Something about the ancient tower enchanted him. In fact, he'd persuaded the forestry division to invest money in its renovation.

A light June breeze tickled the treetops and scattered the thin trails of smoke rising from campfires. The hushed wind stirred his spirit. "God, You're so good." His gaze surveyed the beautiful peaks of the White Mountains.

A couple of young men hiked into his magnified view, and Kavan watched as they made their way along the mountain path.

Setting the binoculars aside, he checked the sky overhead. Clear and blue, no sign of rain. *When did it rain last? Six weeks, maybe,* he thought. It was a little too dry for his liking.

A flash of light nabbed his attention, and with calculated motion, he reached for the binoculars.

A flare. Kavan zeroed in on the area with the binoculars. The white smoky trail led to the general location of the hikers. He grabbed his radio.

"White Birch, this is Donovan. We've got hikers in trouble on the south ridge, 150-foot line. Clear."

The voice of Rick Weber crackled over the radio. "They climbed that high? Go ahead." He sounded dubious.

"Yes. Go ahead."

"I'll send out the chopper. Weber clear."

"Donovan clear." Kavan searched the mountainside for a glimpse of the hikers.

"Kavan," Rick called back in a low voice. "Switch to channel eight five."

Kavan clicked the dial on his radio. "What's up?" he asked.

"When you come in, be ready to rescue yourself from Travis. Rumor has it he's on the warpath over the expenses you submitted."

Kavan exhaled and lowered his arm, letting the binoculars dangle from his right hand while gripping the radio in his left. With a shake of his head, he said, "Thanks. I'm on my way in now."

He took one last glance around the venerable tower before starting for the steps.

Ever since he'd started working on the fire tower refurbishment, his boss, Travis Knight, had scrutinized all his expense reports with a critical eye.

Driving down the mountainside, Kavan recalled the debate he had had with Travis. "You've barely started the project and already I'm getting heat from the division about the expense."

"Travis, I've ordered several hundred board feet of pine and a few large-cell batteries for energy."

"Large-cell batteries? You're wasting division money."

"I planned for the energy cells in the refurbishment budget. Otherwise, we'd have to run power lines to the tower."

Travis shook his head. "I won't have it look as if my office is frivolous with expenses."

"Frivolous? Pine board and batteries are not frivolous." Kavan tried to reason with him, but Travis turned a deaf ear and ordered him to hold off on any more expenses.

Kavan hated the memory of that day. Now, arriving at the office, he dreaded a second confrontation. He addressed Travis's secretary when he entered.

"Hi, Kavan," Cheryl said sweetly, winking at him with mascara-laden lashes.

"Evening, Cheryl. Travis around?"

She tipped her head toward the office door. "Careful, he's in a mood."

"So I've heard." Kavan knocked lightly on the director's door.

"Come in," a deep voice bellowed.

"Evening, Travis," Kavan said, shutting the door behind him.

Travis Knight looked up, the skin under his chin jiggling like jelly. His dark eyes glared at Kavan, and he tossed some papers on the edge of the desk. "What's the meaning of this?"

❧

Elizabeth jogged toward Sinclair's, determined to make it on time. When the short, loud blip of a siren sounded behind her, she jumped off the road with a yelp.

The passenger-side window of a White Birch police car slid down. The officer leaned over and peered up at her. "What are you doing?"

Elizabeth scowled at yet another member of the Lambert family. "Going to work," she said, then added with a thump of her fist on the car door. "What's the big idea of scaring me half to death?"

Her cousin Jeff Simmons gave his wide, teasing grin. "Sorry, Beth, just messing with you."

"You about gave me a heart attack."

"Get in." Jeff pulled the handle and pushed the door open. Elizabeth tossed her backpack inside.

"Why are you jogging to work?" he asked, starting in the direction of the Sinclair's super department store.

Elizabeth hesitated to answer. She loved her cousin Jeff, but if she told him about the tire, he'd do the Lambert family thing and fix it for her. She gave him the first excuse that came to mind. "I need the exercise."

He laughed. "Yeah, right. I saw your car on the side of the road back there."

Elizabeth looked over at her cousin and confessed. "The right front tire blew."

"Ah," he said.

They rode in silence for a minute before she said softly, "Thanks for the lift."

"Lamberts stick together."

"So I've noticed." A wry smile touched her lips.

"A little overwhelming, is it?" Jeff asked, his tone understanding.

"Just a tad. Everywhere I turn, there's a Lambert family member, or worse a family friend, watching me. It's like living in a fishbowl."

"No one's watching you, Beth. The folks in White Birch are just friendly and interested."

"You mean nosy," Elizabeth retorted.

"No, I don't mean nosy." Jeff gave her a sidelong glance. "You like your privacy, don't you?"

Elizabeth laughed and shook her head. "Just a little."

Jeff continued. "I was the opposite when I went to college. Didn't know anyone, struggled with that alone-in-a-crowd feeling. I hated those first few months on campus. I never told anyone, but I think Grandma always knew."

A picture of bighearted Jeff wandering the campus alone caused a wave of mercy to splash Elizabeth's heart. But his situation didn't compare to hers. "I'm the opposite. Grad school can't come soon enough."

Jeff shook his head with a chuckle. "It's the next hill to conquer, is it?"

She twisted her lips to hide a wry grin. "I wouldn't put it like that. . .exactly."

Jeff laughed. "I hope you get the school you want."

"There's no doubt I will," Elizabeth said, confidence rising within her.

"How do you like working for Lambert's Furniture?" Jeff asked, slowing to turn into Sinclair's giant parking lot.

Elizabeth shrugged and looked out the passenger window. "It's a job."

Actually, she enjoyed working at the family business, though she would never admit it. Seeing the business from the inside, she gained a new respect for Lambert ingenuity and vision.

He stopped near the front entrance of Sinclair's. "Here you go."

Elizabeth grabbed her backpack and hopped out of the car. "Thanks, Jeff."

"Anytime, Cousin. Would you like a ride home?"

"No, thanks." She hurried inside and ran past the store's café-style grill. Breathless, she paused long enough to order a grilled ham and cheese. The sandwich waited for her when she came down from the employee locker room.

She ate as she walked toward the front. The evening manager, Joann Floyd, met her in the main aisle. "Take over the customer service desk."

"All right." Elizabeth swallowed the last of the sandwich.

"And can you stay and help me close? MaryAnn called in sick again." Joann fell into step with Elizabeth.

"Sure," she replied, stepping behind the counter and signing into the register. In the past few weeks, the twenty-nine-year-old Joann had become more of a friend than a boss. Elizabeth hated to refuse her request, knowing the extra work would fall to the dedicated manager.

A smile of relief lit Joann's oval face. "Thank you."

Elizabeth shrugged. "What else is there to do in this dinky town?"

Joann answered without preamble. "Meet a nice man, fall in love, get married, have a few kids."

Elizabeth groaned. "You've gone crazy from too much work, Jo. When have you *ever* heard me talk about love, marriage, and kids?" She shook with an exaggerated shudder.

Joann laughed. "Well, I've never heard you talk about it, but it's got to be more fun than grad school."

"You'd rather I stay in White Birch and forget about my plans," Elizabeth said, picking through the basket of returned items.

"Oh no, I don't want you to forget about your plans. I want

you to change them."

Elizabeth chuckled at Joann's forthright confession. "Nothing doing. I'm getting my master's in nuclear engineering, maybe a Ph.D."

"And then what?"

Elizabeth shrugged. "I don't know," she said as Joann headed off to check on a price for a register customer. "I'll cross that bridge when I come to it," she muttered to herself.

For the next hour, the grad–school–bound Lambert handled refunds and sorted the return items. Occasionally Joann walked by, whispering words about love or romance in her ear.

"There are other things in life besides romance," Elizabeth whispered in response.

"I need to return these." A smooth, baritone voice rose from the other side of the counter.

Elizabeth looked up into the chocolate brown eyes of a handsome, uniformed forest ranger. The sparkle in his eyes caused her heartbeat to quicken. Her voice wobbled when she asked, "Do you have a receipt?"

"Right here." He reached into his shirt pocket and pulled out the thin register tape. "After you do the refund, I need to purchase these items again."

Elizabeth peered over the counter and into his cart. It was loaded with all kinds of kids' crafts: poster boards, paints, colored paper, balloons, and sparkles. With an upward glance, she asked, "Whatever for?"

two

For a moment, Kavan felt lost in her large blue eyes. Sapphires set against pure white silk. Realizing he stared, he shifted his gaze and said, "I'm sorry, what did you say?"

She laughed. "You said you wanted to return these items and then purchase them again?"

"Right." Kavan's gaze met hers, and he smiled. "Seems the New Hampshire Division of Forests and Lands can't afford a few balloons and poster board."

Surprise sparked in her eyes. "So you're buying them with your own money?"

"Fun tools make it easy for me to teach the kids about fire safety."

"And our tax dollars don't pay for it?" she asked, incredulous.

Kavan shook his head and said woefully, "Politics."

The lovely brunette behind the service desk recoiled. "Politics? Over kids, crafts and a few balloons?"

"No reasoning for the whims of the politically minded."

"Oh," she said, her lips forming a perfect O.

A distinct desire to get to know the woman behind Sinclair's service counter stirred in Kavan. Casually, he read her name tag: Elizabeth.

About that time, a lighthearted male voice said from over his shoulder, "Here, Beth." A brown paper bag slid across the counter.

"What's this?" she asked, looking past Kavan to the man behind him.

"Dinner. Grandma sent it over."

Kavan watched Elizabeth flare, her face reddening. "I told her that I would. . ."

"Kavan! Hello." A hand clapped on his shoulder.

He turned to the familiar voice. "Jeff." He extended his hand.

"How are you?" Jeff greeted him with a hearty handshake.

"Good. It's been awhile."

"Too long," Jeff said. "I see you've met my cousin Beth."

"No, I haven't had the pleasure." Kavan peered again into her jewel-like eyes.

"Well, let me do the honors. Beth Lambert, meet my old friend, Kavan Donovan. Beth is my cousin from Boston."

Her silky hand slipped into his. "Nice to meet you, Kavan." The melodic sound of her voice speaking his name stunned his heart. "The pleasure is all mine, Beth."

"Elizabeth," she said, pointing to her name tag. "It's Elizabeth."

"Ah yes," Jeff said, a lilt in his voice, "she prefers not to use her country-cousin name."

She eyed him with ire. "Isn't there a crime in town you need to solve?"

Kavan stifled a grin, but Jeff chuckled heartily. "Calm down, Beth; I'm going."

"Here, take this with you." She held out the brown paper bag. "I told Grandma I'd get something to eat, and I did."

"She's just watching out for you," Jeff stated. "When I stopped by Grandpa and Grandma's to see what Gran made for dessert, I told her about your car. She thought maybe you didn't have time to grab that burger you mentioned."

Kavan listened, letting his thoughts linger over the picture of family love and care Jeff's explanation painted. His family life had been very different from that of the Lamberts. Too many lonely nights eating frozen dinners, sitcom reruns his only company.

Moving his thoughts out of the shadowy past, Kavan tuned in to Jeff's monologue. "I got some good news and some bad news about your car."

"My car?" Elizabeth asked while ringing up Kavan's refund.

"The good news is I had your car towed to the garage."

Elizabeth stopped working. "Jeff, you shouldn't have. I can take care of my car."

Jeff held up his hands in surrender. "I know, but I'm family, and I'm helping whether you like it or not."

Elizabeth smiled in defeat. Kavan felt captivated by her beauty. But her precious attention centered on Jeff, not him. "What's the bad news?"

"You need to replace all your tires. Besides the flat right front, the tread is thin on two more, and the fourth one has a nail."

Disappointment etched the elegant planes of her face. "You're kidding, Jeff. How much is that going to cost?"

"Don't worry about it. We'll take care of it."

Elizabeth slammed her hand on the counter, startling Kavan and Jeff. "No you won't." She leaned toward her cousin, waving her index finger in his face. "Don't even try to pull one of your family strings to get me some deal and leave me feeling eternally indebted."

Amused, Kavan watched. He liked the woman's resolve and determination. She didn't think twice about facing down the brawny police officer. Cousin or not, it showed guts.

"All right, all right." Jeff held up his hands. "You're looking at about two hundred dollars."

With a flurry, Elizabeth finished the forestry refund. Kavan engaged Jeff in casual conversation, keeping one eye on the White Birch police officer and one on Elizabeth. He'd been to Sinclair's a thousand times and never seen her before.

When the conversation with Jeff lulled, he heard himself ask the curly-haired brunette, "How long have you worked here?"

"Two weeks." She handed him a credit slip and a pen. "Sign here, and give a reason for the return."

"She's up here from Boston, fresh out of MIT." Jeff spouted more detail. "Came to spend some time with the family. She works for Will over at Lambert's Furniture during the day."

Kavan whistled low and contemplated Elizabeth in a new light. "MIT, I'm impressed."

Jeff's radio suddenly squawked, demanding his attention. "Gotta go. Beth, what time do you get off? I'll come by and pick you up."

"I already told you; I don't need a ride."

"How are you going to get home? Jog? What time do you get off?" Jeff demanded.

"One," she blurted out as if it were a final confession.

Jeff glanced at Kavan with a smirk, then back at his cousin. "I'll see you at one." Jeff headed for the door. Suddenly he stopped and pointed at Kavan. "Have Kavan tell you about the time he saved my life."

ॐ

Elizabeth raised a brow at the broad-shouldered redhead, charmed by his gentle manners and ruddy cheeks. She wondered how he'd saved her cousin's life and why the mere mention of the fact caused a crimson hue to wash over his face.

"You saved Jeff's life?"

"He likes to embarrass me." Kavan fussed with the balloons and construction paper. "I need to buy some other items for the kids, so I'll just check out at one of the registers."

"Have a good night." She studied his straight back as he walked away, disappointed that he no longer stood at the service desk. She liked the ranger, drawn by the kindness and sincerity that emanated from his deep-set eyes.

Elizabeth's musings froze at the sudden realization that Kavan intrigued her. She did not have time for romance or a summer love. Graduate school loomed on her horizon, and she was determined to see her goal to completion.

I'm not stopping five yards short of the goal line. With determination, she shoved her curiosity and attraction for the man aside.

When Joann returned to the service desk from roaming the store, Elizabeth blurted out, "I forbid you to talk about love or romance, Jo."

"Forbid?" Joann echoed, arching a brow. "What sparked that comment?"

"Never mind." Elizabeth exchanged money from one of the cashiers standing in front of the service desk and gave her several rolls of change.

Joann stared at her, one hand on her hip. "I make no promises."

Elizabeth started to reply, but at that moment, eighteen-year-old Millie hurled herself against the counter and asked in a breathless murmur, "Joann, can I please go on break? Mark is meeting me—"

Joann leaned forward and asked in the same breathless whisper, "You two still an item?"

Millie blushed. Elizabeth rolled her eyes.

"Sure, go on," Joann said with flare. "Who am I to stand in the way of true love?"

Elizabeth laughed at the melodrama. "You're ridiculous, you know that?"

"Never," Joann countered with a flip of her hair.

"You take the cake on romance."

"Never mind the cake," Joann said, picking up the clipboard and reading the schedule. "Open register ten so Millie can go on break."

"For you, yes. For love, no," Elizabeth answered with a light laugh and headed for the register.

❧

"So, we meet again." Kavan steered his cart between the magazine rack and the register. He smiled and winked.

A breezy feeling fluttered across her stomach. "I think you are following me, Sir. I'll have you know my cousin is a White Birch police officer." Elizabeth scanned Kavan's items and dropped them into plastic bags.

"Well then, me lady." Kavan bowed with a large sweep of his arm, an Irish lilt to his words. "I'll be minding me manners."

His accent and exaggerated movements made her laugh. "You never told me how you saved Jeff's life."

Kavan swiped his debit card through the checkout terminal to pay for his purchase. "Well, if I told you everything about me, you'd be bored and less inclined to join me for dinner."

Bold. Clever. But as much as the ranger fascinated her, dinner for two might spawn romantic notions, and Elizabeth refused to let her heart, or anyone else's, dictate to her head.

Nevertheless, she didn't want to hurt or embarrass Kavan. Thankfully, she had a legitimate excuse for turning down his offer. "I work most nights." She cashed out his purchase and passed over his receipt.

Slowly, he slipped his debit card into his wallet and reached for the bags. "I see." He paused. "Maybe some night when you're free."

"Maybe." She shrugged, knowing the chances were slim.

"Good night, Elizabeth."

"Good night, Kavan."

≈

On his back porch, Kavan popped the top from a cold bottle of soda. He eased down into a polished oak rocker and set it into motion. Two German shepherds, Fred and Ginger, lay at his feet.

In the distance, a glow of light from the town center burned above the treetops. And on Kavan's kitchen windowsills, oil lamps burned against the darkness.

Overhead, the night sky glistened with starlight, and the songs of crickets filled the air.

Peaceful and reflective, Kavan relived the evening's events. It had been good to see Jeff Simmons. Hard to imagine that they'd once been best friends. Strange how time and life's pursuits changed relationships. He grinned thinking of Jeff's claim that he'd saved his life. Truth of the matter, it'd been the other way around. Jeff saved his life, though it had nothing to do with life *or* death.

An image of Elizabeth crept into his mind and painted warm colors over his thoughts. Growing up in White Birch, the Lambert clan was the closest thing Kavan had to a real family. But somehow, he'd never had the pleasure of meeting Elizabeth. If he had, he was sure he would have remembered.

Standing behind Sinclair's counter, she appeared young and innocent. Jeff's announcement that she graduated from MIT added a whole new dimension to the resolute, blue-eyed woman. He could still hear the slap of her hand on the counter, warning Jeff not to pull any favors to get new tires for her car.

Independent, he thought, *a good attribute for a ranger's wife.*

Just then Fred picked up his head and bayed at the moon. Ginger echoed. Kavan stopped rocking and looked down at them with a furrowed brow. "What? It's okay for you two to have a companion, but not your ole master?"

The shepherds tilted their heads, as if trying to understand. Kavan chuckled and scratched Fred behind the ears. Setting the rocker into motion again, he took a swig of the cola and addressed his Lord in a low, intimate voice. "Only You know what kind of wife I need. I trust You to help me find her."

The shrill ring of the kitchen telephone ignited a barking frenzy. "Settle," Kavan commanded the dogs. "I hear it." He hurried through the back door and reached for the receiver on the third ring.

"Hello." He glanced at the clock. *12:45 A.M.*

"Kavan, it's Jeff. Sorry to call so late."

Kavan grinned. "Seems like old times."

"Well, it'll really seem like old times when I ask you to do me a favor."

Kavan's deep laugh reverberated through the kitchen. "A favor after all these years? It'll cost you."

"Wait 'til you hear the favor." Merriment laced Jeff's words.

"Proceed with caution," Kavan retorted.

"Pick up Beth from Sinclair's for me and take her home. She's living with Grandpa and Grandma."

Kavan slid the mouthpiece away from his mouth and drew a deep breath. His heart thumped in his chest. His reaction to hearing Elizabeth's name surprised him.

"You there?" Jeff asked.

Kavan breathed out slowly. "You're really taking us back to

high school days now, old buddy. I thought you were picking her up."

"I'm processing a domestic violence case and won't get out of here on time. The wife is pressing charges."

"Sad," Kavan managed to say.

"Very. Kids involved. Makes me want to—well, never mind. You going to pick her up or not?"

"With all the Lamberts in this town, you call me?"

"I've never seen any of the Lamberts look at her the way you did tonight. I thought maybe the two of you—"

Kavan blurted out, "Your imagination causes you to see things that aren't there."

Jeff's bass laugh rumbled through the line. "Don't kid a kidder. Can you pick her up?"

Kavan checked the clock again. *Twelve fifty.* If he agreed, he needed to do so quickly. "All right, I'll do it, but you owe me, Simmons. You owe me."

"Thanks, Buddy."

Hanging up, Kavan grabbed his keys and headed for his truck. He regretted not taking the time to clean it out. The seats were covered with dust and dog hair from Fred and Ginger's last ride. Quickly he wiped them with an old but clean rag and started the engine.

Driving to Sinclair's, he imagined what he would say to her. His invitation to dinner met with resistance and little hope for a future date. A nervous twitch ran through him. What if she refused his offer to drive her home? Surely Jeff called and warned her.

Too late now, he thought, turning into the store's parking lot. He spied Elizabeth just inside the doors, leaning against the wall, arms folded, peering out.

"Hi," Kavan said, slowly approaching.

Her eyes showed surprise. "Hi. Kavan, right?"

"Right." He shuffled his feet, feeling awkward. Seven years out of high school and the sight of a pretty lady still made him feel like a clumsy ox.

"Did you forget something? Glue perhaps?" She grinned a saucy grin, exposing white, even teeth.

Kavan laughed. "No, got all the glue I need. Actually, I'm here for you."

Elizabeth stood up straight, though her arms still crossed her petite frame. "For me? Where's Jeff?"

"Tied up with a case. He called and asked if I'd pick you up."

Kavan saw the muscles of her face tighten. And her eyes narrowed. "What is it with this family of mine? They hover and watch. . ." Elizabeth paused, wriggling her fingers in the air as if kneading dough. "I'm sorry Jeff brought you out here at one o'clock in the morning for nothing." With that, she turned and walked back into the store.

Kavan followed her. A tall blond woman behind the counter glanced at him, then at Elizabeth. A mischievous grin spread across her face.

"Joann, can you give me a ride home?" Elizabeth asked.

"Ah, Honey, I live all the way across town. What about your friend here? Hi, I'm Joann Floyd."

"Kavan Donovan." He shook her hand.

Elizabeth protested, motioning to Kavan. "He's a stranger."

Joann winked at him. "But I have plans."

Elizabeth cocked her head to one side and narrowed her eyes. "Sure you do. At one in the morning?"

"My husband rented a movie. Besides, you don't want to make Kavan come all the way out here for nothing."

"I didn't ask him to come out here."

Joann answered with a shrug. She picked up the cash drawer she'd been counting and ducked into the back office.

Elizabeth stared at Kavan, one hand on her hip. With resignation, she said, "Guess you're my ride."

"Jeff should have called to tell you." Certain he saw a sparkle in her blue eyes, he continued. "My truck is right outside. Curbside service."

They walked in silence. Kavan held the passenger door open for her. As she climbed in, she said, "I overreacted.

Seeing you here on Jeff's behalf, well, embarrassed me."

Kavan paused, his hand on the door. "Embarrassed you?"

"Yes, where I come from, one doesn't pick up a stranger from work in the wee hours of the morning."

Kavan pushed the door shut and peered through the open window. "Well," he said, "in White Birch, we do."

three

Elizabeth stretched, stifling a yawn. Flopping against the customer service counter, she faced another mindless night at Sinclair's. Working days at Lambert's Furniture, then evenings and weekends at the super store left her exhausted. And the summer had barely begun.

She glanced up to see Kavan Donovan standing at the service counter, off to one side, watching her. He flashed his lopsided, yet rakish smile.

Instantly, she shot upright and smoothed her hands over her wrinkled smock. Was it her imagination, or were her hands trembling?

Over the past two weeks, Kavan dropped by the store almost every evening. If he didn't, Elizabeth noted his absence with a sharp pang of longing.

"Hi," he said, moving closer.

Elizabeth smiled easily. "What did you forget this time?"

He held up a slender, narrow package, and Elizabeth recognized the familiar toothbrush casing.

"Fred ate mine," Kavan explained.

She gaped at him. "Who's Fred?"

With a deadpan expression, he said, "My dog."

Elizabeth laughed. "Is that anything like 'my dog ate my homework'?" The warmth of his presence wrapped around her heart.

"No, completely different. Not even in the same 'dog eating my stuff' category." Kavan whipped a mangled toothbrush from the pocket of his green khakis.

She inspected the damaged toothbrush. "Hmm."

"Hmm? What's that supposed to mean?" he asked, raising one eyebrow. He placed the new toothbrush on the counter for Elizabeth to scan. "You doubt my story."

"Oh no." She stifled a chuckle. "Sounds perfectly plausible to me. That'll be two fifty-six."

Kavan handed over three ones. "Are you busy tomorrow night?"

"Working again."

"No rest for the weary, eh? Don't they ever give you a night off?"

"Yes, but people call me to work for them, so I do."

"What are you doing with all the money you're making?"

"Spending it on new tires," Elizabeth said with a quick wink, referencing the night they met.

Kavan nodded with a grin.

"Other than that, I'm saving it for my parents," she added.

He furrowed his brow. "You're giving money to your parents?"

"No, I'm proving to them I know the value of a hard-earned dollar. It was my dad's idea, mainly. Send his overachieving daughter back to the family roots, work hard, and take a break from school. I think Dad's afraid I'll turn into an academic with no grasp of day-to-day life. So, I'm. . ." Elizabeth stopped midsentence. She said too much. How did the forthright yet humble ranger rouse her to speak her inner thoughts?

"Working is a worthwhile endeavor," Kavan said in polite response.

"That's what I've been told," Elizabeth said with an edge, handing Kavan his change and toothbrush.

Kavan reached for his purchase and dropped the loose change into a charity basket by the register. "If you have a day off soon, give me a call. Jeff has my number. We could go for pizza."

Elizabeth struggled against the desire to say yes. She was leery of getting close to the man who made her wonder about romantic love for the first time since she was a giggly preteen.

"Have a nice night, Kavan." The ranger turned and walked away. As she watched him leave, a distinguished-looking woman with silver hair and perfect makeup approached the service counter. The customer caught Elizabeth staring.

"He's a handsome one, isn't he?"

Startled, Elizabeth gasped, "Oh, hello, um, may I help you?"

"Kavan Donovan, right?" the woman asked.

Elizabeth stared at the older woman. "He's a friend of my cousin's." Once more, she asked how she could serve the woman.

Instead of announcing what she needed, the woman persisted with the subject of Kavan. "Perhaps a friend of yours, too? A special friend?"

"No!" The word resounded around the service counter like a trumpet blast.

"Too bad," the woman said, moving on to her Sinclair's business.

Elizabeth succinctly finished the transaction, hoping for no more personal prying.

Joann passed by the service area as the woman left with her refund in hand. "Why is it that people are so intrigued with romance?" Elizabeth asked, tossing the woman's returned items into a waiting cart with unusual force.

Her boss stopped. "What are you talking about? What people?"

"Never mind." Elizabeth dismissed the question with a slight wave of her hand. "I'm just tired."

"No, out with it." Joann propped one elbow on the counter. "You got me curious now. Since I'm Queen of Romance—"

Joann's moniker jolted a light laugh out of Elizabeth. She broke down and explained. "Some lady came to the counter as Kavan was leaving and—"

"Ah," Joann interrupted. "This is about Kavan."

"No, it's about why the whole world thinks a young, single female must have a man."

Joann chuckled. "The whole world?"

Elizabeth wrinkled her nose. "You know what I mean."

"Let me ask you a question," Joann started, resting her hand lightly on Elizabeth's arm. "Why are you so adamant against falling in love?"

"I'm not against falling in love. It's fine for most people."

"Just not for you," Joann responded with a shake of her head. "You, my friend, are missing out on one of the best wonders of life. I can't imagine life without David."

Elizabeth didn't know what to say. Since high school, she'd been so busy with academic achievement that love seemed more like a nuisance than a wonder.

When her friends lost all sense of themselves over a cute boy, she plowed ahead with school, making the grade and winning awards. While her friends crumbled with broken hearts, she soared.

During those days, Elizabeth determined never to become one of romance's walking wounded, foiled by the illusions of lasting love.

"You're one of the lucky ones, Joann."

"No luck, Elizabeth. Love. David is a gift from God. And you better be watching, 'cause God just might grace you with the same amazing gift."

Elizabeth sighed. "I'm going on break, Jo."

"Good idea."

&

The golden day faded to twilight blue as Kavan drove down County Road toward home. A New Hampshire summer breeze passed through his open window, and he rested his tanned arm along the door of the truck.

He'd not made his routine stop by Sinclair's to see Elizabeth, though he longed for an excuse to go by the super store. Yet, he needed nothing. His pantry shelves were starting to overflow with superfluous stuff he'd purchased on routine stops by the store to see her and say hello.

Careful, Kavan coached himself. *She'll get wise to you.*

During the past week, he'd run into more Lamberts than he had in the past year. Each one thanked him for helping Jeff a few weeks ago by fetching Elizabeth.

Grandma Betty seemed especially pleased about his acquaintance with her granddaughter. He talked with her one afternoon when she brought several of the great-grandchildren to the state park.

She whispered in his ear, "If that granddaughter of mine would get her head out of the academia clouds for a moment, she'd see what a great catch you are, Kavan Donovan."

Kavan appreciated Grandma Betty's encouragement, but pushing Elizabeth would do the exact opposite of what he wanted. Already she resisted his attempts to get together outside of Sinclair's main aisle. It frustrated him to think she might never surrender to his overtures, though he admired her decisiveness.

No, a clan of Lamberts wouldn't bring Elizabeth into his arms. Only the hand of God could move her heart in his direction.

The blast of a gunshot pealed through the evening air. Kavan slammed on his brakes and stuck his head out the window. He quickly scanned the area.

What's going on?

Another shot cut through the silence. Two white-tailed deer darted across the road followed by two young hunters.

The boys stopped in the road and fired a third time in the direction of the fleeing deer.

Poachers. "Stop!" Kavan jumped out of the truck, incensed.

The poachers swerved at the sound of his voice.

Kavan flashed his forestry badge. "Hunting season starts in November, boys. Put your guns down." He started walking toward them.

The hunters appeared to be in their late teens. They stared at him for a moment, then raced away toward a dark cluster of trees.

"Drop your guns," he hollered, chasing them into the growing shadows. He hurdled rocks and fallen limbs and waded through the thick green forest floor.

As he gained on the poachers, their rusty red pickup came into view.

"Let's go. Let's go," one of the boys yelled, tumbling into

the bed of the truck while the other fumbled with the driver's side door. The engine roared to life.

"You're in violation of New Hampshire hunting ordinances," Kavan bellowed.

The truck accelerated, and the driver aimed it toward a dirt road. Kavan leapt toward the fleeing vehicle, counting on his authority as a ranger to intimidate the young men. "Stop!"

The driver jerked the wheel, grazing Kavan's side with the right front fender. He twisted and turned, trying to maneuver out of the truck's path. He tumbled headfirst down a steep ravine.

Bouncing head over heels toward the bottom, Kavan's knee smacked the ground over and over. Finally, he slid to a stop. The walls of the narrow chasm claimed him like a fortress.

Every part of his body burned and ached. He struggled to stand, but a fiery pain shot through his knee and forced him down again.

"Lord, rescue me," Kavan whispered and slumped to the forest floor. He hoped someone would drive by and see his truck, but few traveled along the side of County Road.

Falling back against the mossy growth covering the forest floor, he set his hand over his head and whispered prayers to Jesus.

❧

Elizabeth woke the next morning, weary. Feeling in a fog, she moved through her morning routine, grateful for her first Sunday off in a long time.

She hated to admit it, but perhaps she did need a break in her schedule. She'd gone straight from studying for finals to working day and night at Lambert's Furniture and Sinclair's.

"Good morning, Beth," Grandma said, catching Elizabeth after she'd showered and dressed. The older woman peered around the door casing of Elizabeth's room.

"Morning, Grandma."

"You look tired, Beth."

"I'm fine, really."

Grandma remained in the doorway. "You can't keep up this pace."

"I've endured worse."

"Perhaps, but even in school you had breaks between terms. A night or two off during the week." Grandma moved to the antique rocker by the bay window.

Elizabeth ran a comb though her wet curls. "I can't remember that far back."

"It's only been a little over a month since you graduated," Grandma chortled.

"Feels like years."

"Well, this old woman here," Grandma paused and tapped her chest with her finger for emphasis, "takes one day a week to literally rest. No cooking, cleaning, or running errands. You should consider doing the same."

"That idea sounds foreign to me, Grandma. I'm used to being on the go, studying, or working on projects. Sitting around seems like a waste of time."

"It's good for the heart and the soul to slow down one day a week, rest, and ponder. I always hear the voice of the Lord so much clearer after a day of no activity." Grandma got up, patted Elizabeth on the arm, and started to leave. She paused at the door. "Your grandpa and I would love for you to come to church with us this morning. Ponder it, and let me know."

Ponder. What a choice word for Grandma to use.

Now that the demand of school was over, Elizabeth had time to ponder things she never had before. During nights at Sinclair's, when the hustle and bustle died down and a hush fell over the store, she allowed her thoughts to dance with images of Kavan and her heart to awaken with love for Jesus. She reveled in childhood memories of Sunday school, comforted by the notion that the Lord loved her.

But ever since high school, her commitment to the Lord remained casual. Instead, she believed more in personal destiny and triumph over the idea of a personal, intimate God.

Elizabeth decided she thought of the handsome Ranger

Donovan far too often. She spent most of her shift on Saturday wishing he'd stop by for a purchase and maybe hang around for awhile. But he never showed.

Grandma stepped into the room again. "Did you decide to join us?"

Elizabeth faced the pretty, plump Lambert matriarch and said, "I'd love to."

"Good," Grandma said with a quick clap of her hands. "Cereal and bread for toast is out on the kitchen counter. Help yourself." She left to get ready.

Elizabeth dressed for church and went downstairs. She poured a small bowl of wheat cereal and sat at the polished cherry table her grandpa made just after the Second World War. Nervous twitters mixed with flashes of excitement about going to church for the first time in awhile.

She took a bite of cold cereal. Grandpa entered the kitchen through the back door.

"Where have you been?" Elizabeth asked, winking.

Grandpa looked at her seriously. "They found Kavan Donovan's truck by the side of the road yesterday afternoon. No one had heard from him in almost twenty-four hours. The Division of Forests and Lands sent out a search-and-rescue team."

Elizabeth dropped her spoon in the cereal bowl. Her heart thumped wildly in her chest. "Did they find him?"

Grandpa nodded. "He climbed out of an eighty-foot ravine on his backside, pulling along a busted knee."

"Is he all right?"

Grandpa reached for a coffee cup and poured. "A little cold and hungry, but he'll live." He sported a saucy grin as he sat down at the table.

"So, you were out helping to rescue him?" Elizabeth asked, spooning another bit of cereal, squirming under her grandpa's stare.

"Me? No, I was taking my morning constitutional. I think it might rain today."

Elizabeth sat back and stared at him. "Then why'd you make it sound as if he was still missing when you came in the door?"

"I just wanted to see the look on your face. They rescued Kavan last night."

"Har, har. You're a regular riot, Grandpa. A regular riot."

"You looked pretty flustered."

"Well, of course. You come in here somberly announcing that a man is missing."

"Oh, I beg to differ. Not just any man. Kavan Donovan."

Elizabeth rapped her knuckles lightly on the table. "You haven't gone senile on me, have you, Grandpa? Why would Kavan Donovan be more important to me than anyone else?" she bantered.

"You tell me? Handsome forest ranger, single, loves the Lord. . . Has a nice home up off I-89. . ."

Elizabeth sighed. Gazing into her grandpa's twinkling eyes, she shook her spoon under his nose. "I have two words for you, Grandpa: graduate school. Can you say 'graduate school'?"

"Oh sure," he said, shifting sideways in his chair and slinging one arm over the back. "Grad-u-ate school. But can you say 'true love'? 'Kavan'?"

"Honestly! What is with this town and romance? It's like reliving junior high school."

"What are you two going on about?" Grandma asked as she entered the large, airy kitchen.

"I hate to tell you, Grandma, but Grandpa has finally gone senile."

Grandma laughed and played along. "Well, then, guess we'd better get going to church so the preaching can give your grandpa the sound mind of Christ. Matt, hurry and change."

He pushed away from the table. "Two words, Bethy, two words: 'Kavan Donovan.'"

Laughing, Elizabeth tossed a wadded-up paper napkin after the older man. "How do you put up with him, Grandma?"

"Love. More than sixty years' worth."

The word sank into Elizabeth's soul like a pebble in the

sand. *Love.* How could one simple, four-letter word pack so much power?

A verse from her Sunday school days flashed across her mind. *For God so loved the world. . .*

Elizabeth studied her grandparents for a moment, realizing how much a part of each other they'd become. The lines of their individuality blurred so that it had become hard to define where one stopped and the other began. The two had become one.

She shook her head, trying to loosen the hold her thoughts were taking on her soul. A love like her grandparents', no matter how beautiful, was too much for her. She preferred the independent life of a single woman. It was heart safe.

On the drive to church, Grandma serenaded her with hymns. Grandpa sang along, his bass harmony supporting Grandma's clear, wispy melody.

Inside the sanctuary, Grandpa led them to a pew already filled with Lambert children and grandchildren. Feeling a bit overwhelmed, Elizabeth opted to sit in the back alone.

As the pastor stood to call the congregation to worship, a warm masculine voice whispered over her shoulder. "Is this seat taken?"

four

Kavan slipped in beside Elizabeth before she had a chance to respond. Stiff and sore, he slowly sat down and settled his crutches in the aisle alongside the pew.

"What are you doing here?" Elizabeth whispered. Her blue eyes focused on his bandaged knee as she scooted over an inch or two.

"It's Sunday," he whispered back. "Time to worship the Lord with the rest of the saints."

"You're hurt!"

Kavan slipped his arm along the back of the pew and leaned in toward Elizabeth. "Hurt, not dead."

"How did you get here? You didn't drive, did you?"

"Got a ride from a good Samaritan."

The three children sitting in front of Kavan and Elizabeth stole a peek at them. Their mother motioned for them to face forward with a fast flick of her wrist, then gave Kavan and Elizabeth a stern, you-should-know-better glance.

Elizabeth hid a laugh behind her slender hand.

"Shh," Kavan said softly into her ear, "you're setting a bad example for the children."

Elizabeth answered him with a dark blue-eyed wink. The urge to envelop the delicate woman in an embrace almost overwhelmed him.

Elizabeth Lambert, someday you'll be mine. Before God and man. Someday.

From the front of the sanctuary, the worship leader strummed the first chords of the opening song on his guitar. "Let's stand and worship the Lord," he said.

Awkwardly, Kavan tried to rise. His damaged knee throbbed with pain. To his surprise, Elizabeth slipped her hand into his and aided him to his feet.

"You don't have to stand, you know. I think people will understand."

Kavan leaned on the forward pew for support. "Feels good to stretch," he said in a low voice. He kept a light grip on Elizabeth's hand, loving the touch of her soft skin against his. He didn't want her to feel obligated to hold on to him, so he relaxed his fingers a little more so she could let go anytime she wanted.

Yet, her hand remained in his, eyes fixed forward, her smooth contralto voice rising in worship.

Smiling, Kavan offered thanks to his Lord and King, his Friend. Last night in the ravine was a reminder of the Lord's love and protection. His injuries could have been severe. Worse, the poachers might have returned, realizing he could identify them.

What an awesome God You are, he thought.

Elizabeth's hand still clung to his even after worship and the offering, until Pastor Marlow stood at the pulpit, his Bible open. "Glad to see Kavan Donovan with us this morning," he said first thing, motioning to the back where Kavan sat with Elizabeth. "For those of you who don't know—"

Kavan listened as the pastor shared the details of his ordeal. With a sidelong gaze, he watched Elizabeth. A crimson hue spread across her pretty face. All eyes were on them. She moved her hand out of his and nestled it in her lap.

Across the way, Jeff Simmons smiled broadly and waved. *I'll never hear the end of this one.* He hoped none of the Lamberts had seen him holding Elizabeth's hand. He'd rather take a ribbing about being bested by a couple of poachers than have Elizabeth scared off by good-natured teasing.

"Today's text is John, chapter three," Pastor Marlow said after concluding Kavan's story.

Throughout the congregation, pages rustled. Kavan opened his Bible to the Gospel of John.

"Here," he said to Elizabeth, sharing the open book with her.

She smiled shyly, glancing first at him, then at his Bible. Kavan longed to know the thoughts running through the private, independent Lambert granddaughter's mind. Did she enjoy worship? Sitting next to him? Did the pastor's focus on him embarrass her? Would she ever hold his hand again?

Kavan leaned back against the pew and tried to control his rambling thoughts. But the violet scent of Elizabeth's perfume filled his nostrils like the aroma of a cool spring morning just after a rain.

Suddenly, he realized this was the first time he'd seen Elizabeth outside of Sinclair's. The first time he'd seen her in anything other than a green smock and black khakis. He yearned to spend time with her outside the walls of Sinclair's store.

But how?

" 'For God so loved the world,' " Pastor Marlow read from John 3:16.

Concentrate on the preaching, Donovan. This is the Lord's time.

After the sermon, Kavan turned to Elizabeth. "Thanks for helping me stand earlier."

She smiled but averted her gaze. "No problem. I'm glad you're okay."

"I was thinking maybe we could have lunch—"

"Kavan," Jeff called over his shoulder. "You're looking none the worse for wear."

Kavan turned awkwardly to face his friend, disappointed at the interruption. "I'm banged up, but I'll live." He watched Elizabeth out of the corner of his eye.

"Listen, come to the station tomorrow and give us some details on the guys you were chasing. We'll round them up and—"

Elizabeth's lovely, low voice interrupted. "Grandpa is motioning for me. I'd better go. Bye, Kavan. See you later, Jeff."

Leaning on his crutch, Kavan waved good-bye, then gave Jeff a light pop on the shoulder with his fist. "Thanks, Man. Thanks for nothing."

Jeff stared at him wide-eyed. "What? What'd I do?"

Chuckling, Kavan eased down the aisle toward the door. "Ruined my lunch."

❧

There she stood holding his hand. Unbelievable.

Why didn't you move your hand, Elizabeth? she chided herself.

She couldn't get the picture out of her head. Standing next to Kavan with her hand in his—and in the middle of a church service!

All morning while logging purchase orders at Lambert's Furniture, the image of her hand in Kavan's flashed past her mind's eye over and over until she thought she could actually feel the strong, warm curve of his palm enfolding hers.

It felt divine, like a soft pair of kid gloves she once tried on during a Manhattan shopping spree with her mother.

Truth be told, she didn't know how her hand got into his. He attempted to stand for worship, and without much thought, she reached to help him. Simple as that.

She wondered if anyone saw them. Well, if anyone she knew saw them. The whole town knew her anyway, so what did it matter?

How humiliating. Elizabeth plopped her head onto the desk.

"Beth? You okay?"

She jerked her head up, smoothing her hair with her hand. "I'm fine, Will. Fine. Just thinking."

Her cousin and boss chuckled. "Try not to think so hard."

Elizabeth wrinkled her nose. "I'll try."

Will started to walk away, but stopped short. "See you up at the homestead this Friday for the barbecue?"

"What? Oh, Grandpa and Grandma's barbecue. I'm working at Sinclair's that night."

Leaning against the door frame, his hands in his pockets, Will shook his head. "No you don't. Take the night off. Have some fun with the family."

The look in his dark blue eyes persuaded her. "I'll see what I can do."

"Good."

Once again, Elizabeth faced the pile of work, determined to focus on the task at hand. She clicked the left mouse button to open the next account, New Hampshire Division of Forests and Lands.

Ranger Kavan Donovan's face popped into her thoughts again. Beneath the bruises and scrapes, his brown eyes laughed and his smile possessed the world.

I've got to think of something besides him! Elizabeth pushed away from her desk and snatched up her coffee cup. She started for the door, but changed her mind. Diet soda. *Umm, sounds good.*

She opened her bottom desk drawer and fished her wallet from her purse. *Fifty cents, can of soda. Oh, and a candy bar. Midmorning snack is what I need—anything to get my mind off of Kavan Donovan.*

Elizabeth dug out another quarter, two dimes, and a nickel. Dropping her wallet back into her purse, she glanced at her computer to check the time.

Her eye caught the next purchase order on the stack. Kavan Donovan's name was scrawled across the bottom of the order in bold letters. Elizabeth sank into her chair.

She scanned the order that totaled one thousand eight hundred thirty-seven dollars. "Hmm, five hundred twenty-five feet board of. . ." Elizabeth scanned the page, then checked the invoice on the computer, muttering to herself. "Cherry?"

No wonder Kavan's boss took issue over a few paints and balloons for a kids' display. What was he doing buying expensive lumber for the forestry division?

Elizabeth sat back, the change for the soda and candy machine sticking to her palm. After a moment, she reached for the phone and dialed Grant Hansen, the production floor manager.

"Hi, Mr. Hansen, it's Elizabeth."

"Beth, what can I do for you?"

Elizabeth liked the deep resonance of the older man's

voice. "Do we fill lumber orders for people? You know, order the wood without making it into furniture?"

Grant laughed. "I see you've run across our little company secret. We have customers from the old lumberyard days that we still service."

"Do we fulfill orders for the forestry division?"

"On occasion. Maybe for a special repair or construction project."

"Cherry?"

With a chuckle, Grant answered, "No, no. Not for the forestry division. Cherry's very pricey. We use it here for fine furniture."

"I see," Elizabeth said, fighting a rise of disappointment. Why would Kavan order expensive lumber for the forestry division?

"Everything okay, Beth?"

She hesitated. "Yes, Mr. Hansen. Thanks for your help."

෯

For Kavan, turning into Matt and Betty Lambert's driveway Friday night felt like a homecoming. How many nights and weekends had he spent at the Lamberts' home on the hill, as he called it, during his childhood and teen years? He and Jeff had pitched their tent on the crest of the hill many a summer night. Remembering, he smiled.

He parked his truck and stepped out.

"Kavan!" Ethan Lambert greeted him with a hearty hug before calling to his wife. "Julie, come say hi to Kavan."

Jeff beckoned to him from across the lawn, waving large barbecue tongs. The smell of roasting meat rose up from the wide barbecue pit and wafted on the wind across the lawn. Kavan's mouth watered.

"You're just in time, my friend," Jeff hollered.

Kavan scanned the grounds for signs of Elizabeth, his heart beating slightly faster at the idea of seeing her.

Suddenly, a soft voice greeted him. Turning, he looked into the delicate green eyes of Jeff's sister, Heather Simmons.

"Well, Heather. Hello." He gave her a light hug. "It's been a long time."

Heather agreed that it'd been too long since they'd seen one another. Then, she introduced her husband, Thom. "It's Heather Barrett now, by the way."

Kavan positioned himself on his crutches so he could shake Thom's hand. "A pleasure to meet you."

"And this is Baby Barrett," Heather said, patting her round belly.

"Congratulations," Kavan said, kissing Heather's cheek tenderly. He'd never been particularly close to Heather, but on several occasions during high school, they found themselves in deep, heart-to-heart conversations. She would always be special to him for that reason.

Betty Lambert came alongside him and rested her hand gently on his arm. "Why don't you sit down? I'll get you a plate." She winked at him like she knew a deep secret.

"Grandma Betty, I don't need you waiting on me. I can manage."

"Oh, now, I see you hobbling around. I won't have my good barbecue falling on the ground and going to waste."

Kavan laughed. "Well, then I accept your offer."

He made his way over to one of the long picnic tables and eased down to the plank bench, searching again for Elizabeth. Surely she had to be here. It appeared to him that every Lambert in White Birch was in attendance.

"I didn't know you were invited."

Kavan did an about-face at the sound of Elizabeth's voice. The sight of her took his breath away. The setting sun laced her brown curls with golden ribbons. The blue sparkle in her eyes made him feel both hot and cold. She smiled at him as if she knew what she was doing to him.

He said the first thing that came to mind. "So, Sinclair's gave you the night off?"

"I had no choice." She picked up his crutches and rested her underarms on the padded tops. "Between Will and

Grandma, I couldn't say no to this family event."

"You look lovely," he said in a low tone.

"Will said he'd fire me from Lambert's Furniture if I didn't come tonight," Elizabeth continued. She put the crutches back and settled against the edge of the picnic table.

"Good for him."

"Thank you."

Kavan smiled. "You've lost me. 'Thank you' for what?"

"The compliment."

"Anytime," he said, locking his gaze with hers.

She let it linger, but only for a second. "I heard Jeff tell Grandpa that they may have found the poachers who knocked you down the ravine."

"Turns out a detective knew one of the boys from my description."

"Ah, the woes of a small town. Can't commit a decent crime. Everyone knows you."

Kavan's smile faded. "Don't be fooled," he warned. "People get away with stuff around here all the time. Problem is they pat you on the back in church on Sunday, then steal from you on Monday."

Elizabeth's posture seemed to stiffen. "Is that so?"

He nodded. "Unfortunately. But let's not talk about poachers and White Birch crime." Kavan paused, studying her face, trying to read her expression. "Let's talk about going for pizza."

"I don't date." Elizabeth stooped to pick a yellow dandelion and twirled the green stem between her thumb and forefinger.

"What? Pizza with a friend is not a date."

"It's the classic date," she said with a harrumph. "Boy meets girl. Boy hounds girl at her place of employment. Boy asks her to go for pizza and a soda."

"Hound you? Come on, Elizabeth, give me a break. Besides, I never said anything about a soda."

She made a face at him.

He laughed.

"Here you go." Grandma Betty passed between the two of them, placing a heaping plate of food in front of Kavan. She stepped back, surveying the two of them. "Having fun?" she asked, buoyancy in her voice.

"Tons," Elizabeth droned.

"We were enjoying ourselves until I asked her to go for pizza," Kavan admitted without preamble.

In a way that only Grandma Betty could, she encouraged Elizabeth. "Go for pizza. You might surprise yourself and have a good time."

Kavan held his breath for a moment. Elizabeth sighed. When she turned toward him, a whirlwind of butterflies seemed to explode in his stomach.

"How's Monday night?"

"I'll pick you up at six."

"Six-thirty," she countered.

Kavan chuckled. "Six-thirty it is."

"My job here is done," Grandma Betty said, brushing her hands together as she started back up the hill toward the food tables.

five

All day Monday, the pizza date with Kavan proved to be an utter distraction to Elizabeth.

She set an empty coffeepot on the burner and scorched the bottom. Will asked her for the week's receivables, and she delivered last year's. When the phone rang, she answered, "Sinclair's," and at lunch she noticed she had on one black pump and one navy.

"What's up with you today?" Will wondered, leaning against the doorjamb.

She smirked. "Marauding Monday."

Will stepped into her office and dropped into an empty chair. "Anything bothering you?"

Part of her wanted to come clean and cry, "Oh, Will, I have a *date* tonight!" But the words crumbled in her mind. How could she have ever agreed to have pizza with Kavan? But it wasn't a date, right? Kavan said as much, just pizza and a cola.

"Nervous about tonight?" His hushed voice conveyed his tenderness.

"Tonight?" Elizabeth echoed. Shifting in her seat, she pretended to read E-mail though her inbox was empty.

"Pizza with Kavan?"

"What is with this family?" She slapped the desk. "Everyone knows everyone else's business."

Will raised his hands in defense. "We look out for each other, support each other, and cheer each other on."

Elizabeth shuffled papers around, keeping her gaze averted. Will's piercing gaze made her feel vulnerable as if he could read her sacred thoughts. "I'm not used to it. Mom and Dad raised Jonathan and me to be independent and self-reliant." She forced herself to look up at him.

"Don't kid yourself, Beth. Grandpa and Grandma raised all the Lambert kids to be independent and self-reliant. Where do you think your parents got the idea?"

"Some things in life are just meant to be personal, that's all, Will."

He got up to leave. "Some things in life are meant to be celebrated."

⋆

Kavan hit a wall of tension Monday morning.

"He's in a mood," Cheryl warned.

Kavan sighed. He didn't want Travis Knight's state of mind to spoil his day. The pizza date with Elizabeth was foremost in his own mind. During his morning workout, he'd barely been able to keep his mind focused on lifting the weights properly without overworking his knee. Now that he was using a cane instead of crutches, he wanted to keep it that way.

Taking in a deep breath, Kavan entered his boss's office.

"Morning. Is there a problem, Travis?" Kavan settled in the chair across from Travis's desk.

The large man jerked with irritation. "The refurbishment money. What are you buying, Donovan, gold-plated screws and platinum nails?"

The refurbishment budget again? He hadn't done anything with the project since Travis had ordered him to stop spending. "I don't understand."

Travis leaned toward Kavan, his mud-brown eyes narrow with indignation. "I'm getting heat from accounting. This is government money you're spending, Donovan."

Kavan stood carefully, leaning heavily on the cane. "Heat for what?"

"Outrageous charges to the refurbishment account." Travis rattled a report under Kavan's nose.

"I've barely spent any money." Kavan hated being on the defensive.

"Not according to accounting's records." Travis rose to his

feet and settled his plump hand on his plump hip.

Kavan circled the chair, running his free hand over his hair. "I don't like what you are inferring, Travis."

"Then stop spending money that isn't yours." Travis pounded the desk.

"What are you talking about?" Kavan turned toward the man. "Are you accusing me of stealing?"

Travis shook his head, his fleshy cheeks red with heat. "I'm not accusing you of anything." He paused, then added with force, "Yet."

Hearing all he could bear to hear, Kavan looked his superior in the eye. "I'm not stealing, and you know it."

"Then explain these reports indicating that we are overbudget on lumber and supplies. That's your department, Kavan."

Kavan picked up the report and scanned pages. After a moment, he tossed it back onto the desk. "Those are just department numbers and totals, Travis. It reveals nothing."

"All the red numbers are under your department, Kavan."

Kavan pursed his lips, holding his answer. When his anger subsided, he said, "I'm not spending the money."

"I won't have my career toppled by your carelessness. I'm up for promotion, and this doesn't look good for me."

Whether Travis Knight dismissed him or Kavan walked out, he couldn't remember. He sat at his desk feeling as if he'd been sucker punched.

Cheryl sashayed by. "I told you he was in a mood."

Lord, what's going on? Kavan pushed away from his desk, grabbed his keys, and headed for his truck. He needed a quiet place to pray.

Driving out of town, Kavan wrestled with anger and disappointment. His solid relationship with Travis had been the reason he returned to the New Hampshire Division of Forests and Lands. Now the man challenged his integrity. Kavan prayed with purpose until peace settled over his soul.

Ahead, the White Birch covered bridge came into view. Rays of morning sunlight scattered diamonds of light across the surface of the White Birch River.

Kavan parked and slowly walked under the bridge's cover, letting the tension of the morning ease out of his mind. His thoughts wandered to his evening plans with Elizabeth.

A picture of her shiny curls and intense gaze made him smile for the first time all morning.

ঌ

Will's words echoed in Elizabeth's mind. *Some things are meant to be celebrated.*

I'll tell you what's to be celebrated, she thought with scorn. *Achievement. Certainly not a pizza date. What did an old bachelor like Will Adams know anyway?*

Elizabeth pounded the keyboard, entering new invoices for faxed purchase orders. How could this family get so excited over two people sharing a large pie of tomato sauce and cheese?

She liked Kavan all right. In fact, she might like him more if the family didn't meddle. Then there was Joann. Her Sinclair's boss called on Sunday to see if she could fill in Monday night. When Elizabeth said no, Joann insisted on a reason.

"I see." Joann's tone turned serious when Elizabeth caved and told her about her plans with Kavan. But she hardly fooled Elizabeth, who could hear the smile in the woman's reply.

"I don't even know why I'm doing this," Elizabeth muttered under her breath, getting up to file a stack of invoices. The idea of canceling appealed to her. Hadn't she always promised herself she'd avoid romantic entanglements until the end of grad school, maybe longer?

She regretted the agreement with her parents to live and work in White Birch. She felt as if she were losing momentum on the education front. All would be lost if she let her heart fall in love.

She picked up several invoices and slipped them into a folder and shut the file drawer. Back at her desk, she found the phone book in a cubicle on the credenza and looked up Kavan's number. She dialed and listened as his answering machine picked up.

"Hi, Kavan, it's me, Elizabeth." She paused to steady her voice. "I, um, well, I can't make it tonight. I'm really sorry. I appreciate you asking and all. See you around."

She hung up.

Some things in life are not to be celebrated.

&

After resting in God's peace, Kavan left the covered bridge and headed up I-89 toward the White Mountains and the old White Birch fire tower. Parking at the base of the fire tower, he left his truck and headed over to the tower steps. Carefully he eased his steps around the old rotting boards, placing his feet firmly on the bright clean pine steps.

He examined the tower structure, climbing slowly, leaning heavily on the cane. A lot of work remained to be done. Kavan knew there was no way for this refurbishment project to be overbudget.

At the top of the tower, he pulled out the binoculars and scanned the area.

The panoramic view before him deepened his sense of peace. Nevertheless, something about the ordeal with Travis bugged him. "I don't know how to fix this, Father. I need Your wisdom." He continued to release his concerned thoughts to the Lord. After a few minutes, Kavan understood the need to surrender his reputation to the Lord, trusting Him to guard it.

A warm breeze whistled through the broken boards of the fire tower roof. Kavan faced the wind and sighed with contentment. He thought of Elizabeth and reached for his cell phone, dialing the main number for Lambert's Furniture.

"Elizabeth Lambert, please," he spoke to the receptionist.

When she answered, his heart thumped.

"Elizabeth, it's Kavan."

&

Sinking into her chair, Elizabeth took a deep breath. "Hi."

"Pepperoni or cheese?"

"Where are you?"

"Up at the old fire tower."

"I see."

"So, what kind of pizza do you like? Pepperoni, cheese, veggie. . . ?"

Absently, she reached for a pencil and doodled on the edge of a piece of paper. "Cheese, I guess."

"Sounds good. Six-thirty?"

She swallowed. "Six-thirty."

Why didn't I just tell him? Now I'll have to explain my message. A knot tied Elizabeth's stomach. She was giving this whole event entirely too much mental and emotional energy.

☙

Getting ready that evening, Elizabeth heard her grandma fussing around in the hallway, singing the same tune over and over.

"It's no big deal, Grandma. Just pizza," she called.

Grandma peered around the door frame. "Did you say something?"

Elizabeth's laugh filled the room. "I know you're hanging around in the hall, waiting for me to come out."

The older woman stepped into the room, her face lit with a smile. "You look very nice."

"Thank you."

"Can I give you some advice?"

Elizabeth pursed her lips and tipped her head to one side. "And if I say no, will that stop you?" She couldn't keep her serious expression and smiled.

"Doubtful." Grandma pulled out the desk chair and sat down. "Have fun, Bethy."

Elizabeth reached for a pair of small, blue diamond earrings. "I just wish everyone wouldn't make such a big deal about this."

"Everyone?"

"Everyone," Elizabeth repeated. "You, Grandpa, Jeff. . . Even Will knows."

"I mentioned it to him. Sorry." Grandma got up and stood behind Elizabeth, brushing her hair from her shoulder. "You've been so intent in your studies. It's okay to let go a little and see how the other half lives."

"Perhaps celebrate?" Elizabeth asked, using Will's word. She turned and faced Grandma. She was so beautiful with her carefully combed silver hair and steady blue gaze.

"Yes, celebrate."

"I'll try not to be too stoical and serious," Elizabeth consented with a smile.

"That's my girl," Grandma said with a hug.

Elizabeth glanced at the clock. She had a few minutes before Kavan would arrive. She checked her E-mail. A half dozen junk E-mails, which she deleted, a couple science E-newsletters, and one personal note from a friend filled her inbox.

> *Elizabeth, good news! I've decided on Ohio State's nuke engineering program. Have you heard yet? Let me know. It would be great if we ended up in the same program.*
> *Hope you're having fun in New Hampshire.*
>
> *Jenna*

Despair sank into the pit of Elizabeth's stomach like a lead weight. No, she hadn't heard from any schools. Surely, she should have heard something by now. What was it Jenna wrote? Elizabeth reread the E-mail.

I've decided on Ohio State's nuke engineering program.

"She must have had several schools to choose from," Elizabeth whispered. "But not one school has contacted me."

Slipping on a pair of black, low-heeled ankle boots, she mentally reviewed the application process, sure she'd met every requirement. She'd carefully prepared for grad school submissions, not wanting to get rejected due to a technicality.

"Beth, what are you doing?" Grandma's voice startled Elizabeth. "Kavan is waiting."

Consumed in thought and fighting worry, Elizabeth missed the tenor sound of the doorbell ringing.

Elizabeth buried her head in her hands. "I can't go!"

six

Kavan stood in the Lamberts' sunny living room, angled to one side, propped up by his cane.

Grandpa Matt made small talk and asked about his knee.

"It's a little sore, but healing nicely. Cane works well."

"That's wonderful." Matt Lambert leaned back in his chair.

Elizabeth seemed to be taking a long time to come down, and he wondered if she'd changed her mind.

"Hi, Kavan. Sorry to keep you waiting."

He turned at the sound of her voice, unable to suppress his smile. Dressed in a faded pair of jeans and a pullover, he thought she looked perfect.

"No problem." He hobbled over to her and whispered, "You look absolutely beautiful."

"Thank you," she whispered back. "Night, Grandpa. Night, Grandma."

"Good night, folks." Kavan waved back as he opened the door.

On the drive to Giuseppe's Pizza, he attempted to start a conversation with Elizabeth, but all his topics fell flat. He could see worry in her blue eyes. The couple remained silent for the rest of the drive and to the front door of the restaurant.

"Table for two," he told the hostess who greeted them.

Once they were seated and their drink order was taken, he studied Elizabeth's face for a second, then took the plunge. "What's bothering you, Elizabeth?"

She sat up a little straighter and her brow furrowed. A slight smile molded her lips. "Didn't know I was wearing my heart on my sleeve."

Kavan laughed. "It's right out there, about to fall off." He motioned to her arm.

50

The waitress set two tall glasses of fizzing soda before them. "What'll you have?" She glanced between Kavan and Elizabeth.

"I think we need a few more minutes," Kavan said after making eye contact with Elizabeth. He felt certain she had not considered what she wanted to eat.

"I'm sorry, Kavan. I. . .uh—"

"Hey, Elizabeth," Kavan interrupted, "let's order, then we can talk about it over pizza."

The way she smiled made his insides shiver. They agreed to order a large supreme pizza with no olives. The waitress chewed a big wad of gum and blew a giant bubble before asking, "Is that all?"

As she walked away, cracking her gum, Kavan and Elizabeth shared a laugh. "I'll be sure to leave her a big tip." Kavan sipped his soda.

"Do that. I needed a good laugh." Elizabeth swirled her straw in her glass.

"What's on your mind, Lambert?" Kavan settled back, prepared to listen.

"I read an E-mail from a friend just before you came to pick me up. She's already decided on a grad program, and I have yet to hear from any of the five schools I applied to."

"It's really important to you, isn't it?"

Elizabeth nodded, and her chin jutted out in determination. "Very. It's what I've planned to do since I was a teenager. The nuclear engineering field is wide open right now, especially for women."

"A lot of money in engineering."

Elizabeth agreed. "Most of my friends are satisfied with their bachelor's and are not going for their master's. I, however, refuse to go the traditional route because some biological clock tells me it's time for marriage and kids. I'm not falling for that old routine."

Kavan didn't miss the edge in her voice, her unspoken resolution to go against the grain. He idly fiddled with his fork and said, "Sounds like you have your life planned out."

Elizabeth gazed out of the window by their booth, a grin accenting her pretty face. "My dad used to tell me I could do anything I set my mind to. He helped me set goals. So far, I've achieved them all."

No goals for marriage and family, Kavan noted. He repositioned himself in the seat, poised to ask her about her future family plans when the waitress returned to refill their drinks. She plopped a basket of garlic knots onto the table. "Your pizza will be out in a few minutes."

Elizabeth reached for a knot and placed it on her plate. "Obtaining my master's degree is my next major achievement." She looked up at him. "Can't ruin my perfect record."

"No, I guess not." Kavan reached for a garlic knot. Funny how the thing he admired most about Elizabeth was the very thing that would keep them apart. "I remember waiting to find out about grad school—"

"You went to grad school?" Elizabeth's eyes were wide with surprise.

"Uh-huh. University of Maine."

"I didn't know one could get an advanced degree in your field."

Kavan looked at her, astounded. "Well, forestry is—"

Her soft laugh interrupted him. "I'm just kidding, Kavan."

He laughed. "You had me there for a minute." He took another swig of his soda.

"I should warn you about my weird sense of humor."

The waitress returned with a large pizza pie. "Here ya go." She set down two white plates and slipped a large slice on each one.

Kavan thanked her and returned his attention to Elizabeth. "I actually got my master's degree in math." He bit into his slice of pizza.

Across the table, Elizabeth gaped at him. "Really?"

Kavan reached for his napkin and wiped his mouth. "I like math and actually thought teaching would be a good backup career."

"Name your favorite math course." Elizabeth propped one elbow on the table and reached for her pizza slice.

"Diffy Q."

Elizabeth made a face. "Differential equations? No way! I hated Diffy Q. Give me advanced dynamics or any physics course over Diffy Q or calc three."

"Advanced dynamics! Are you kidding me?" Kavan countered. "I attempted some of those courses as an undergrad and realized life was just too short."

Like alto chimes, Elizabeth's laugh filled the air. "I love anything to do with physics, figuring out how things work and why. I actually love robotics. The math, for me, is a means to an end."

Kavan responded, arguing the beauties of mathematics and with almost no effort, their conversation took flight, gliding gently on the wind of words.

❧

Elizabeth picked up a third big slice of pizza. "Giuseppe's has the best pie."

Kavan agreed. "I loved coming here as a kid."

"You did?" Elizabeth regarded him. The news of his mathematics master's degree put him in a new light. She didn't deny it—she was impressed. With little effort, she found she liked him and appreciated his comfortable company. "What's your favorite childhood memory?"

Kavan paused. The glimmer in his eyes seemed to dim. "Probably coming here. Or winter Sundays at your grandparents' house."

"I see."

Clearing his throat, Kavan confessed, "I came along a little later in life than my parents anticipated."

Elizabeth leaned over her plate, poised for another bite of pizza. "Is that a bad thing?" She pulled a melted strand of cheese from her chin.

Kavan hesitated before answering. "Not necessarily." He took a long, slow sip of soda.

"Listen, Kavan, you don't have to talk about it if it's too personal."

He played with his fork again, tapping it on the table. "I don't mind, really. Most people in town know about my parents. They are good people, but they liked to travel."

"They didn't take you with them?"

"No. Every woman in town over the age of sixteen baby-sat me at one time or another." Kavan made a comical face, causing Elizabeth to chuckle.

"That's amazing."

"Your grandparents' place was my favorite. They always made me feel like a part of the family."

"That's how you and Jeff became friends?"

"Yep."

"In the course of things, he saved your life?"

Kavan jabbed his straw into the melting ice of his empty glass, a sly grin spreading across his face. "I'm not sure I remember all the details."

"Ah, don't keep me in suspense." Elizabeth moaned, tipping her head to one side. "Don't you know curiosity killed that cat? Think what it will do to an inquisitive electrical engineer like me."

A laugh rumbled from the ranger. "I'm telling you, I can't remember."

"Oh, sure." She put on her best pout.

"Tell you what, give me a few days, and I'll see if I can remember."

"Deal."

Silence dropped over them like a thin veil. Elizabeth relaxed and thought the lull necessary. Like exhaling after holding her breath.

"Didn't I hear you had a brother?" she said absently.

Kavan nodded. "He's twelve years older than I."

"So, you were like an only child."

Kavan nodded. "Only and lonely."

The inflection in his voice moved Elizabeth. It resonated

with a sad, yet resolute tone. Obvious to her, Kavan did not crave sympathy. It seemed he'd come to terms with the condition of his childhood.

"Where are your parents now?"

"Europe. Paris in spring is my mother's favorite. They'll return to the States sometime this summer. They go to Florida a lot." He smiled.

To herself, Elizabeth resolved to appreciate her family more. She'd spent most of her teen years running here and there, desperate to grow up, hungry for independence.

"What about your family?" Kavan's rich voice interrupted her thoughts.

She grinned. "I was just thinking of them and how I didn't appreciate them enough."

"I see. Take it from me, appreciate them."

Resting her folded arms on the table, Elizabeth looked Kavan in the eyes and confessed, "White Birch is a difficult place for me. There's a Lambert, or so it seems, under every rock, around every corner."

Kavan laughed outright.

Elizabeth slapped her hand lightly on the table. "It's not funny."

He chided her. "Oh, come on. It is funny. You can't seriously be offended at your caring, giving family."

"They're meddlers, getting in everyone's business."

"Like Jeff trying to help you with your car."

"Exactly." She pointed her finger at him.

He raised his hands in surrender. "All I can say is, learn to love it. There's no greater feeling in the world than family."

The waitress returned, still snapping her gum. "Refill on your drinks?"

"Please," Kavan answered for both of them. He leaned toward Elizabeth, cocked his head to one side, and raised his right eyebrow. "Dessert? They make a great torte."

Before Elizabeth could answer, the waitress said, "I'll bring a dessert menu." Popping her gum, she turned away.

The two laughed again. "Really, Kavan, big tip for her. She's hilarious."

He grew serious. "I'm having a good time."

Elizabeth stared at her empty plate, somewhat unnerved by his forthright confession. "This place is a great," she said after a moment, forcing herself to look up and into his eyes.

The waitress returned, and they ordered dessert: one chocolate torte with two forks. After that, the conversation drifted back to family matters. Kavan took another stab at trying to get her to see the value of a close family. She understood, but argued that too much closeness can turn into interference.

"I guess we have to agree to disagree," he finally said, shoving the dessert plate toward Elizabeth. "You have the last bite."

"It's a matter of perspective, Kavan," Elizabeth started, spearing the last morsel of torte. "You want what you never had: a close family. I want to be on my own, living my own life. Grad school is the last key to unlocking that door."

"Can't argue with you there, Elizabeth. But I don't think God meant us to do it all on our own. Independence can be a dangerous thing."

Elizabeth wiped her mouth with the edge of her napkin. "I'll keep that in mind."

The waitress brought the check, and Kavan signed. Elizabeth had already noted he was a southpaw and watched as he signed his name on the debit card receipt with a flurry and a flare.

"Nice signature, Kavan," she said, peering over the pile of plates and used napkins. "Think your *K* is big enough?" She glanced up at him, winked, and laughed. "It's unique, I'll give you that!"

"Do you want to pay for dinner?" He raised a brow at her.

"I might." She lifted her chin to accept the challenge.

He chuckled and reached for his cane, anchored in the corner of the booth. "That's it. We're out of here."

To her surprise, Elizabeth let him take her by the arm and lead her toward the door.

Driving toward the Lamberts' home on the hill, Kavan tried not to process the events of the evening too much. But unless he missed his guess, Elizabeth was having a good time. She gripped his heart each time he was with her.

"Sorry I started out the evening so moody," she said.

He reached over and touched her arm tenderly. "Don't worry. I understand. Hang in there; you'll hear from those grad schools."

"I know, but time is passing and I'm getting anxious."

"I bet you'll hear something by the end of the week."

She smiled at him. He wanted to capture her light and bottle it. On bad days, he could pour himself a cup.

"Your optimism is infectious. And you're right; I'll hear soon."

The White Birch covered bridge came into view. Kavan pulled off and asked Elizabeth if she'd like to go for a walk.

"I'd love to if your knee isn't too sore."

"It's fine. Let's go."

She stepped out of the passenger side of the truck into the full light of the moon.

Kavan fished his flashlight out of the glove box and came alongside Elizabeth. He tucked the flashlight under his arm, leaning on his cane as they walked. Without contemplation, he reached for Elizabeth's hand, glancing sideways at her to catch her reaction. She walked steadily forward, her hand resting in his.

They walked in silence, the night resonating with the sound of their heels and the tap of his cane against the broad boards of the bridge floor.

"It's so peaceful here." A contented sigh escaped Elizabeth's lips.

"Great place to pray because it's so peaceful," Kavan added. He released Elizabeth's hand and moved to the middle of the bridge. Moonlight streamed through the small side windows, but he clicked on his flashlight nevertheless. "When we were kids, we liked to climb into the rafters." He moved the light beam up along the heavy support planks.

"Look at all the initials." Elizabeth stared up, turning in a slow circle. "There must be hundreds of them."

"Your grandparents' initials are in here somewhere." Kavan stepped toward the left end of the bridge. "Your grandpa showed me once, but I can't. . . Ah, here it is."

Elizabeth hurried over to where Kavan stood. At the end of his light she read, "ML loves BC 1940."

"Used to be all the engaged couples came here and carved their initials." Kavan took a step back and bumped right into Elizabeth. When he turned to apologize, her face was only inches from his. His heart thundered, and he swallowed hard, finding it difficult to breathe. *Kiss her*, his heart shouted. She was gazing at him.

"Well, it's late," he choked out after a moment. "I'd better get you home." He took one giant step back. *Kiss her?* he argued internally. *How can I kiss her? This isn't even supposed to be a date.*

"Right," she answered in a hushed tone. "I have to work tomorrow."

"Me, too."

His legs trembled slightly as he escorted Elizabeth to the truck, a passionate tension wafting in the air between them. The debate over whether he should have kissed her raged on in his mind.

At the Lamberts' door, he grasped her hand and shook it good night. "I had a great time. You're a fun pizza partner."

She stepped toward him. "I had a great time, too."

The moment lingered, and Kavan could feel a light sweat beading on his forehead. "Good night, Elizabeth."

He stepped back so quickly, he stumbled down the front porch steps.

"Kavan!"

"I'm all right, I'm all right," he shouted, getting his balance and hustling to his truck.

"Are you sure?" she called.

The melodious sound of her voice lingered in his ears as he headed toward home.

❧

Inside, Elizabeth leaned against the front door. Grandma called from the family room. "That you, Bethy?"

"Yes, it's me."

"Did you have a nice time?"

Lovely. "Yes."

Suddenly feeling self-conscious, Elizabeth hurried quietly up the front stairs. In her room, she shut the door and flopped onto her bed.

He almost kissed me!

seven

The next morning, Elizabeth hurried down to breakfast. She'd overslept, forgetting to set her alarm the night before. The smell of eggs, bacon, and coffee teased her senses before she entered the kitchen.

Grandpa peered at her over the top of his paper. "Must have been some date. . ."

Elizabeth halted him with a flash of her palm. "It was *not* a date, Grandpa."

"I see." He snapped the paper open again and retreated behind the front page.

"Grandpa," she started with a sigh, "I didn't mean to be sharp with you. I forgot to set my alarm, so I'm running late."

He set the paper aside. "Bethy, did you have a nice time?"

She fumbled around the kitchen, looking for her favorite glass. "Yes."

Grandma came into the kitchen. "Your glass is in the dishwasher. I ran it last night."

"Thank you." Elizabeth retrieved the tall, wide-mouth glass, filled it with ice, and popped open a diet soda.

"That's all I wanted to know," Grandpa said. "Having a good time is half the battle for you."

"I know how to have a good time." Elizabeth pulled out a chair and sat down at the kitchen table.

Grandpa chuckled and sat back, scratching his head. "I suppose you do. You just seem so opposed to it."

Grandma set a plate of eggs and toast in front of her. "Oh, Grandma, I'm not hungry."

"Eat," the older woman ordered. "You're not leaving my kitchen with diet soda as your breakfast."

The smell of hot buttered toast stirred Elizabeth's appetite.

Her stomach grumbled. She reached for her fork and knife. Grandpa passed her the black raspberry jelly.

"I'm not opposed to a good time, Grandpa," Elizabeth said after swallowing a bite of her eggs. "I am merely cautious of my emotional energy."

Grandpa uttered a low harrumph. "I suppose the Allied forces of World War Two couldn't stop that stubborn pride of yours."

Elizabeth spread an even layer of jelly on her second piece of toast. "Stubborn pride? And where do you suppose I get it?" There was a tender admiration in her question.

Before Grandpa could answer, Grandma brought her own plate to the table and interrupted. "All right, you two. Stop. Matt, leave the girl be." She turned to her granddaughter. "You know we're both very proud of you. You're a joy to us."

"Thank you, Grandma."

Grandpa sat back and crossed his arms over his chest. "She's right, Kitten. I just hate to see you all wound up with this grad school notion."

Elizabeth smiled at him, deciding more debate was pointless. She may resist the Lamberts' constant intrusion, but she couldn't ask for more love and support than her grandparents gave her. They tolerated what they didn't understand, loved amid difficulty.

"Why don't you tell us about your dinner with Kavan," Grandma prompted. "No comments from you, Grandpa."

He held up his hands in surrender. "Not a word. Not a word. The floor is yours, Bethy."

She glanced at her watch. "Okay, here's the five-minute version." Quickly, Elizabeth recapped her evening, giving them the details, devoid of any emotion. She omitted the intimate moment on the bridge entirely. Unsure of what really transpired between them in that instant when they were face-to-face and eye-to-eye, she was sure she could not describe it to her grandparents. Besides, the moment felt private, only for her.

"Well, good," Grandpa said when she finished. He picked up the morning paper again.

"Sounds lovely," Grandma chimed in.

On her way to Lambert's Furniture, Elizabeth's thoughts remained caught on the covered bridge moment with Kavan. Did he want to kiss her? Did she want him to kiss her? She shuddered with realization.

As she pulled into the parking lot and made her way to her office, Elizabeth resolved to stop thinking of Kavan Donovan and his possible kisses.

Focus, Elizabeth, focus. Your goal is grad school. Not to marry the first guy who comes along.

❧

Kavan sat on his back porch, sipping coffee and watching the summer mist dissipate over the White Mountains. Fred and Ginger lay at his feet. Content and peaceful, he conversed with his heavenly Father.

He woke up thinking of Elizabeth, and it concerned him some. "Lord, I don't want to get ahead of You. Clearly, Elizabeth is not ready for a serious relationship, let alone marriage. If she is not for me, let me know."

He paused, listening, waiting for the Lord to respond. He did, but not about Elizabeth. Instead, he sensed the Lord warning him about the workday ahead.

More trouble.

Kavan spent the next twenty minutes praying for his boss and the situation between them. He went to work with a sense of God's favor and justice but with no clue as to what events would unfold during the day.

"Morning, Kavan," Cheryl said, batting her heavy black lashes. She smiled at him in a way that made him uncomfortable and wonder what she was thinking. "Travis wants to see you."

Kavan sighed and dropped his canvas bag onto his desk. Taking a deep breath, he limped toward Travis's office.

"Come in," the director bellowed at Kavan's light knock.

Kavan planted a smile on his face and stepped inside. "Good morning."

The large man stood. "We have to figure out how to solve this problem."

Exasperated, Kavan asked, "What problem, Travis?" He eased into a chair.

"Since our last discussion, nothing's changed. Your fire tower renovation is still way over budget."

Kavan clenched his jaw and consciously tried not to grind his teeth. "Travis, I haven't been working on the renovation. There are no expenses."

Travis tossed the accounting notice to him. "Can you explain this?"

Kavan picked up the paper. "This report has no details. It's just a summary. I can tell you my accounting shows the project in the black." He tossed the paper back onto the desk.

"The State of New Hampshire shows you're in the red." His tone challenged Kavan.

Kavan folded his hands on the curved head of the cane and leaned forward, extending his own challenge. "How long have you known me?"

Travis shrugged. "Since you were a kid."

"Do you really think I would steal from the division?"

"People change, Kavan."

"I haven't changed, Travis. I am not the reason the refurbishment budget is overdrawn."

For a moment, Kavan believed he could actually cut the tension with a knife. *Lord, give me wisdom.* "You're free to look at my records, Travis."

The man shook his head. "Won't do any good. Accounting can just say you doctored your records."

"I have copies of orders and receipts." Kavan held his tongue from declaring this whole thing an outrage.

"Whatever it is you're doing, end it now, Donovan. I don't want to see you in trouble."

Kavan left the office without being dismissed. Anger

brewed in his chest. How could Travis believe he was stealing?

He booted up his computer and launched the fire tower refurbishment accounting program. To his anguish, the program came up with an application error. He double-clicked on the program shortcut to launch it again, but it crashed.

He pursed his lips and pounded the palm of his hand against his desk. *Backups. . . I have a backup at home.*

He grabbed his gear and started for the door.

"See ya, Kavan," Cheryl called after him.

At home, Kavan found his records were several months behind, but in order, showing his project to be in the black. A few purchases were not logged in the spreadsheet, but all copies of the project's orders and receipts were saved in a file at the office.

For a few moments, Kavan sat mulling over his next action. Fred and Ginger whined at the door, asking to be let in. Still lost in thought, Kavan got up and opened the door for them.

How do I handle this, Lord?

Oddly, Kavan sensed he wasn't to do anything. He had to let the Lord defend him. For a moment, the idea went against every instinct in his body, but the Lord would handle the situation righteously and justly.

"My reputation is on the line, Father," Kavan prayed. "But I trust You." He'd keep his records in order and updated. When Travis called for them, he'd be ready.

Driving back to the office, Kavan finally rested in the peace of the Lord. Thoughts of Elizabeth drifted across his mind for the first time since the confrontation with Travis.

Ironic, he thought. This morning, she was the first person he thought of when he woke up. Now, after the ordeal with Travis, their pizza dinner and walk on the bridge felt like a distant memory.

❧

"You're crazy not to fall for him," Joann told her over a large garden salad at the diner.

"Why do I have to fall for him? For anyone?" Elizabeth

stabbed a large tomato wedge with her fork.

"I'm not saying you do, but Kavan Donovan is not one to let go."

For the rest of lunch, Elizabeth steered the conversation away from the topic of love and Kavan. She whispered a prayer of thanks when Joann let the subject drop.

After lunch, a pile of invoices and corresponding purchase orders covered Elizabeth's desk. She'd managed to put Kavan out of her mind during her morning routine—but not since her impromptu lunch with Joann. Facing an afternoon of mundane work, she found herself daydreaming about the handsome ranger. Joann was right. He was a great guy: kind and caring, funny, smart, and good-looking.

He would be a wonderful husband and, I bet, a good father. But I'm not looking for a husband or a father for my children! She scooted up to her desk and reached for the invoices.

After updating several accounts, Elizabeth came across another expensive purchase order from the Division of Forests and Lands for one hundred board foot of teak.

Kavan's name sat boldly across the header of the invoice. On the purchase order, his signature graced the bottom line.

She reached for the phone and called Grant Hansen again. "Hi, Mr. Hansen, it's me."

"What can I do for you, Bethy?"

"Would the forestry division order teak?"

He chuckled softly. "No, no."

Elizabeth scanned the order. "It says it's for the fire tower refurbishment."

"Oh no, Honey. The fire tower would be finished with pine or oak."

Elizabeth could feel her heart sinking. What was Kavan doing buying teak? "Thank you, Mr. Hansen," she said low and unsure.

Driving to Sinclair's that night, Elizabeth could not stop thinking about the order in Kavan's name. *Could he be a fraud? Perhaps he's not the man everyone believes him to be.*

Joann caught her as she entered the store. "Hey, your man is in here."

Elizabeth froze. "What?"

"I said your man is in the store." Joann linked her arm through Elizabeth's and steered her toward the time clock. "Clock in. I need you at the front desk."

"No, I can't see him."

"Who? Your man?"

With force, Elizabeth said, "Would you stop saying that? He's *not* my man."

Joann reared back. "Don't get testy. So, he's not your man."

Elizabeth clocked in, then grabbed her friend by the arms. "Joann, I don't want to see Kavan right now. This whole ordeal is ridiculous. I'm not becoming involved. I'm going to school in two months."

Resolve pursed Joann's lips. "All right, Elizabeth. I hear you."

"No more Kavan. No more love talk. No more romance."

Joann reached out and smoothed Elizabeth's curls. "Why don't you work back stock for awhile. Millie can help at the front desk."

With a sigh of relief, Elizabeth hugged her boss. "Call me when he's gone."

From over her shoulder, Kavan's mellow baritone filled her ears. "Hi, Elizabeth."

eight

Elizabeth whipped around. "Hi. . .Kavan."

"I'll see you later." Joann retreated.

"Long workday?" Kavan asked, pushing his cart out of the way so another customer could get by.

"I'm used to it." She avoided direct eye contact.

"Elizabeth, what's wrong?" Kavan's eyes searched her face.

She leaned her shoulder against the wall and fidgeted with the pen dangling from a string by the time clock. In the distance, she heard the cry of a small child. Finally, she looked at Kavan. "I don't want last night to mean more than it should." There, she said it.

"Pizza and a walk on the covered bridge. Don't see how any deep thing could be derived from that experience."

"Oh, you know this town, my family. . . Romance is all they think about."

Kavan shook his head. "Believe me, not everyone in this town is fascinated with romance. You can ask your police officer cousin about that."

"All right, but where I'm concerned, everyone is fascinated with romance. Trying to marry me off."

Kavan took a step back. "Have you been asked?"

Elizabeth stood straight and stared into Kavan's eyes. "What?"

"Who's asked you to marry him?" His eyes sparked with merriment.

"Well, I haven't been asked." She started to laugh.

"Then stop worrying about it. I've known you only a short time, but you are clearly the most goal-oriented, determined woman I've ever met. A little teasing about romance is not going to drive you off the road of educational success."

67

"You're right!" Elizabeth threw her arms around him. "Oh, Kavan, thank you!"

❧

Sunday morning, Kavan found Elizabeth sitting by herself in the back of the sanctuary. He slipped into the pew beside her, hooking his cane over the seat in front of them.

"Good morning," he whispered.

She faced him, her eyes clear and bright. "Morning, Kavan."

He hesitated, then asked, "Do you mind if I sit here?"

"Of course not." She flashed her wide, white grin.

Kavan eased back against the pew, waving and greeting people as they passed. He glanced at Elizabeth from time to time, watching her expression, looking for signs of being uncomfortable. She appeared relaxed and at ease.

Five days had passed since the night she threw her arms around him in Sinclair's. But he could still feel the warmth of her skin touching his neck and smell the fragrance of her perfume.

He'd deliberately left her alone the rest of the week. If they were going to have any sort of relationship, Elizabeth had to feel safe.

The worship leader took the platform and called the congregation to worship. For a brief second, Kavan still wished he had his crutches so Elizabeth could help him stand. He rather enjoyed holding her hand.

"Need me to help you stand?" she whispered.

"I think I can manage." He grinned. *Ah, she remembered.*

His voice mingled with hers as they sang praises to the King. During the offering, Kavan got an inspiration.

"Hey, Elizabeth," he whispered.

She shushed him, but a smile edged her lips.

He reached for the pen in his coat pocket and wrote on the bulletin, "Lunch? My place?"

He passed the paper to her.

She read it and wrote one word: "Okay."

❧

Sitting next to Kavan and among the members of White

Birch Community Church, Elizabeth felt oddly at home. After that first Sunday she agreed to attend with her grandparents, she knew spiritual strength was missing in her life.

"Let's open our Bibles to John 15," Pastor Marlow said.

Elizabeth reached for her Bible and thumbed to the passage. She could hear the rustling pages of Kavan's Bible.

"Book of John," he muttered. "One of my favorites."

"Apparently, the pastor's too."

Forty-five minutes later when the pastor closed with prayer, the words of Jesus danced through her head. *"I have called you friends."*

Could she be Jesus' friend? Lately, He seemed more like a faraway entity that watched the world with vague indifference. Maybe He intervened in times of war or disaster, but did He really care and intimately watch over individuals like her?

In that instant, her soul yearned to know the Lord deeper. Tears stung in her eyes. "Jesus," she whispered so low she could barely hear her own words, "I'd like to be Your friend."

Her shoulders hunched forward as gentle sobs took control. Without a word, Kavan slipped his arm around her shoulders and stuffed a tissue between her fingers.

❧

The Lambert family gathered at the door after the service. Grandpa chased the youngest grandchildren in a game of tag, and Grandma organized lunch out.

"Where to?" she asked in a strong but caring voice.

Ethan and Julie said they preferred lunch at home. Will said he was up for pizza or a hamburger plate at the diner.

"Ah, no way," someone shouted. "Typical bachelor fare."

"What about you, Beth?" Jeff asked.

"I have lunch plans." Her heart pounded an extra beat. *Please don't ask with whom.*

"Beth's out," Grandma said, "so how many are going on this adventure?"

A chorus of young voices cried, "Me!"

The adults laughed. Grandma made a command decision.

"Pizza it is. Let's go."

While everyone scurried to their cars, Elizabeth shook her head with wonder. She had a wonderful family, a little wacky at times and nosy, but so loving and kind.

In the distance, she saw Kavan waiting by his truck. He waved. For the first time, she saw him as a true friend. He didn't push or pry. His comment to her the other night in Sinclair's practically revolutionized her White Birch world. Who cared what everyone else thought?

"Let's go; I'm starving," he called, still leaning against the truck, his arms folded over his chest. The rust color of his tie brought out the ruddy hues of his complexion.

"I'll pull around behind you so I can follow," Elizabeth hollered to him, starting for her car on the other side of the parking lot. Slipping in behind the wheel, she realized she had two new friends today: Jesus and Kavan.

❧

"Oh, Kavan, your place is beautiful." Elizabeth walked through the main room toward the kitchen. Thick open beams criss-crossed over her head, supporting a large open loft that looked into the living area and kitchen. A white stone fireplace sat in the south wall, framed by large-paned windows.

"Thank you. It's taken awhile, but I'm finally getting it finished."

Elizabeth turned with a start. "You built this yourself?"

"Yes." Kavan opened the porch door. "Fred, Ginger. Come." Two large German shepherds bolted through the door.

Kavan joined Elizabeth in the middle of the room. The dogs followed, sniffing Elizabeth, their tails wagging. "The big one with the black face is Fred. And this lovely lady is his mate, Ginger."

With a sideways glance and a smirk, Elizabeth said, "Clever names! Do they dance as well as Fred Astaire and Ginger Rogers?"

Kavan laughed and scratched behind Fred's ears. "Nah; I just watched a lot of old movies growing up. Anyway, most of this room has been done for several years. But I'm finishing the loft and the porch."

Before Elizabeth could comment, Kavan slapped his hands together and said, "I'm hungry. How about you?"

She rested her hand on her stomach. "Starved."

"Couple of rib eyes cooked on the grill and a salad suit your appetite?" Kavan pulled the meat and salad fixings out of the refrigerator.

"Sounds perfect. How 'bout I make the salad while you cook the steaks."

He grinned. She liked his lopsided smile. It reminded her of a young 1950s movie star.

"We make a good team, Lambert," he said.

She nodded. "Good friends are hard to find."

He looked up at her, paused in midmotion. "Yes," he said. "Good friends are hard to find."

nine

"Two letters came for you today," Grandma said when Elizabeth came in after a Saturday shift at Sinclair's.

"Really?" A nervous shudder ran over her. " 'Letter' letters or grad school letters?"

"Official-looking letters," Grandma said. "I put them on your desk."

Elizabeth took the stairs to her room two at a time. In the fading light from the window, she saw two long white envelopes on the desk. She clicked on the desk light. With anticipation, she reached for the top letter.

She mumbled to herself as she read. "We regret to inform you that your application has been denied."

She reread the line. *Denied.* Slowly she sat in the desk chair. Trembling fingers reached for the next letter.

Denied again.

"I can't believe it. I've been turned down by Michigan and South Carolina."

Fighting tears, she paced her room, trying to console herself. *It's only two schools.* She'd applied to five and only one needed to accept. Surely one of the remaining schools would respond positively.

Grandma appeared in the doorway. "Beth?"

"I got turned down."

"I see."

"I, uh. . ." Elizabeth's voice broke. She rushed past her grandmother and down the stairs.

"Hey there, Kitten," Grandpa called from the family room.

Without responding, Elizabeth opened the front door and ran across the lawn. By the time she reached the covered bridge, she was out of breath. Beads of sweat trickled down her cheek and neck. She walked the length of the bridge, contemplating her situation. A June breeze whistled through the eaves.

Denied. She visualized the word over and over. Tears stung in her eyes, but she sniffed them back, refusing to give in. "I won't cry. I know I'll get accepted at another school."

She exited the bridge on the other side and stood along the riverbank, listening to the soothing sound of the water. Jesus' words from Sunday's sermon whispered through her. *"I have called you friends."*

In the fading light of the setting sun, Elizabeth eased to the ground. "Jesus, I could use a friend right now."

Finally, she let the tears spill over and slip down her cheeks. "I know this is not the end of the world, but it sure feels like it. My plans are not working out."

She wiped her cheeks with the back of her hand, wondering how the Lord would respond to her. As a little girl, she pictured herself running up to Jesus like the children in the Bible. But now she felt old and stale, unable to run to her Savior.

Suddenly, a burst of anger riveted her. How could she *not* be accepted? Her credentials were stellar. If anyone qualified for a nuclear engineering graduate program, she did.

Yet, the anger faded as rapidly as it'd flared and disappointment surged again. She longed to shake the heavy burden that wrapped up her heart. "Lord," she said after a few minutes, "I want to be Your friend. Be my friend, please. Show me what to do in this situation."

Twilight settled over White Birch and grace over Elizabeth Lambert.

❧

"She worked during the day," Joann Floyd told Kavan.

He rapped his knuckles against Sinclair's customer service counter. "Thanks." He turned to leave.

"Hey, Kavan," Joann called after him. "Don't give up on her."

He paused, looking at Joann over his shoulder. "She doesn't make it easy."

Joann nodded. Kavan could tell she understood Elizabeth

quite well. "She knows what she wants," the Sinclair's manager said.

"I can't fault her. I know what I want, too."

Joann came out from behind the counter and walked toward Kavan. "Elizabeth Lambert?"

He stepped away from her. "That's for me to know and you to find out."

Joann's laughter followed him out of the store.

He drove toward the Lamberts' home on the hill. He wasn't sure what he would do once he got there, but he headed there anyway. Normally, he'd knock on the door, confident of a warm welcome by Grandpa Matt and Grandma Betty. But now that Elizabeth lived there, he wondered if his impromptu visit would make her uncomfortable.

His Sunday lunch with her had gone well. Better than he'd hoped. But Elizabeth Lambert held strictly to the business of being friends. Only friends.

Steering around the bend in the road, the White Birch covered bridge came into view. In the fading twilight, Kavan thought the truck's headlights flashed across someone sitting on the riverbank. He slowed as he approached the bridge and leaned over the steering wheel. Peering out the windshield, he saw her. *Elizabeth.*

He popped his head out the open window. "You fishing?"

She jumped up, flicking leaves and dirt from her jeans. "Kavan. Hi," she said with a quick wave.

"I don't see a pole or a line." It was nearly dark, but in the remaining light he could see she'd been crying.

He parked in a gravel spot at the side of the road just before the opening of the bridge, cut the truck engine, and grabbed the flashlight. "Hey, hey," Kavan said tenderly, slipping out of the driver's seat and meeting Elizabeth by the bridge. "Everything okay?"

In one smooth motion, he wrapped his arms around her and pulled her to him. She cried while he stroked her hair and murmured to her that everything was going to be okay.

"Elizabeth, tell me what's going on." He inclined his head to look at her. "Why all the tears?" He reached for his handkerchief and gave it to her.

She wiped her face and blew her nose. With a steady voice, she confessed, "I received two letters from universities today."

Kavan stood straight. *News from grad schools. . .here goes.*

"What'd they say?" He smiled to encourage her.

"I was denied admittance."

For a split second, Kavan wanted to rejoice. But he knew better than to give way to his own selfish desires. Elizabeth needed his friendship and support right now. "Who turned you down?"

"What does it matter, Kavan?" she asked, stepping out of his embrace. "That's two less chances I have." She started toward the covered bridge.

"You have all the credentials, Elizabeth. You know you do."

"Apparently not enough for Michigan or South Carolina."

"Why don't you inquire?"

"No, I'm not going to go crawling to them. I have three other applications out there. I'll get accepted at one of those schools."

Kavan gave her a sly smile. Her attitude reflected the Elizabeth Lambert he was getting to know. He walked up behind her and touched her shoulder. "I'm sure you will."

"I've never had to deal with this before. I usually get what I want, when I want."

"Anything I can do to help?"

She faced him. He could see her lower lip tremble. "No, there's nothing you can do, really." Her weak tone told him otherwise.

He stepped closer and wrapped her in his embrace again. She rested her head against his chest. For the longest time, they just stood under the peaceful cover of the bridge.

At last Kavan prayed, "Lord, You know all things. You have Elizabeth's welfare on Your heart. You have plans for her good and not to harm her. Give her Your grace during this time and bless her."

Elizabeth whispered, "Amen," then tilted her head to look at him, still snuggled against his chest. "He's my Friend, you know."

"Jesus?"

"Yes, Jesus. And He sent you to me tonight."

At that moment, emotion for her almost overwhelmed him. He longed to whisper in her ear that he loved her. Slow and determined, he tipped his head toward her, intent on kissing her this time.

But just as his lips were about to touch hers, flashing red and blue lights illuminated the bridge and the loud bleep of a siren reverberated.

"Beth, is that you?"

Elizabeth jumped out of his arms. Kavan squinted in the light.

"Jeff?" he called.

"Kavan? Sorry to disturb you, Man. I was looking for my cousin Beth."

"Here I am," Elizabeth said, her voice cracking.

From where he stood, Kavan couldn't see Jeff's face, but he knew the man was grinning from ear to ear when he said, "Oh, really now."

❧

Suspended between emotions, Elizabeth didn't know whether to laugh or cry. She rubbed her forehead with her fingers. "What are you doing here, Jeff?"

"Grandma called. Asked me to look for you."

A wave of guilt washed over her. "Oh, Jeff, please tell her I'm fine, and I'm sorry."

His deep laugh echoed down the bridge. "I will. Kavan, you see she gets home safely, huh?" Jeff ducked back into the squad car.

"Oh, great. Now the whole family is going to wonder what I was doing out here with you."

"You worry too much about what they think," Kavan said matter-of-factly.

She rested her hands on her hips. "Don't hassle me Donovan; it's been a hard night."

"I know. I'm sorry."

Elizabeth peered up at him. The white glow from his flashlight illuminated the area where they stood. What a wonderful friend he'd become. His comfort tonight was just what she needed.

Thank You, Jesus, for being my Friend and for sending Kavan to be Your arms and voice.

Kavan tapped her on the arm. "Here, use my cell phone to call Grandma Betty so she doesn't worry."

Reaching for the phone, Elizabeth thanked him. She dialed home and waited for an answer. "Hi, Grandma. . . . Yes, I'm fine. . . . I'm sorry I made you worry. . . . Uh-huh, Jeff found us. Kavan is here."

She listened to her grandma's soft, caring voice. "I've been praying for you. I think Jesus just wants you to know He's there for you to lean upon."

The words moved over Elizabeth's heart and invoked a fresh batch of tears. "Thank you, Grandma. I think you are right."

She pressed the END button and handed the phone back to Kavan. He enveloped her again and settled his arm on her shoulders. "You know, whatever doesn't kill you will only make you stronger."

She laughed. "Well, those are comforting words."

"I just mean—"

"I know what you mean, and you're right." She chuckled low.

"Hey, did you notice I'm sans cane?" Kavan said, pointing to his healing knee.

Elizabeth clapped her hands softly. "Yea, good for you!"

Kavan did a jig around the bridge floor. Elizabeth laughed, and it felt good. The wind whipped through the bridge, stirring up dirt and leaves.

"Kavan," she said suddenly, "let me see your handkerchief again. Something's in my eye."

Her eye stung and watered as she slid the white cotton

cloth under her eye, hoping to mop up any remaining mascara or dirt. The edge of the fabric touched the inside of her right eye, and the sting worsened. "Oh, this hurts!" She stooped over and covered her watering eye with her hand. Debris rubbed against her contact lens.

Kavan knelt next to her. "Elizabeth, what's wrong?"

"My contact lens." She tried to open her eye, but the lens had repositioned and stuck to her eyelid, making it impossible to open.

"What can I do to help?"

"Nothing. Just a sec. . ." Elizabeth massaged her eye with her fingertips, trying to move the circular plastic piece. "I wear gas permeable lenses. And if it moves off the pupil, it really hurts."

She tried one more time to move the lens, just wanting it out of her eye. Suddenly the lens slipped into place, and Elizabeth popped it out of her eye with a quick blink. *Ah, relief.* Just as the lens hit the palm of her hand, the evening breeze gusted through the covered bridge.

Kavan laughed. "It's like a wind tunnel."

"Don't move!" Elizabeth commanded. "My lens dropped out of my hand."

"You've got to be kidding," Kavan said, frozen in place, shining his flashlight around their feet.

"I thought I heard it hit."

They looked for over half an hour before realizing the lens must have slipped through one of the cracks on the bridge floor.

"I'm sorry," Kavan said, making one last sweep with his light.

Elizabeth looked at him, one eye pushed shut. "I appreciate your help."

He ran his forefinger tenderly over her lensless eye. "Do you have a spare set?"

She shook her head. "One of the things I didn't get to between graduation and coming up here."

"How are you going to see to drive or work?"

"I have a good pair of glasses here. I'll have to go to Boston to get new contacts."

"Come on, I'll drive you home."

Elizabeth walked with Kavan to his truck. He opened the passenger door, and she paused before climbing in.

"Thank you for being so patient and kind." Without contemplating the implications, she rose up on her tiptoes and kissed him tenderly on the cheek.

ten

After church the next day, Elizabeth started for Boston. She rolled the window down and propped her elbow on the door. The sun burned warm on her bare arm. She beeped the VW's horn good-bye to her grandparents, who stood in the driveway, waving. Grandma's apron billowed in the breeze.

On the passenger seat, a fresh-baked loaf of banana bread filled the entire car with the sweet smell of all that is good in life.

At the bottom of the drive, she turned left, heading for the bridge and the road toward Boston. Just as she crossed the covered bridge, she saw Kavan's truck parked in the shade.

She steered her little car next to his big truck. Kavan still wore his Sunday shirt and tie, but the tie hung loose about his neck. He propped his hand on the steering wheel and leaned out the open window.

Her heart fluttered. "Surprised to see you here." She ignored the excitement stirring within her.

"I wanted to say good-bye again."

His tone caused a funny feeling to bubble up in her middle, and she squirmed under his intense stare. "I'll only be gone a few days."

He shrugged. "I know, but I'll miss you."

Miss me? She didn't know what to say. While growing to appreciate and value Kavan's friendship, it hadn't occurred to her that he would miss her. She pushed her glasses up on her nose and said the first thing that came to mind. "We can go to Giuseppe's when I get back."

"You're on."

She shifted the tiny car into gear. "Bye, Donovan."

"Bye, Lambert." He grinned, flashing white, even teeth.

Driving away, a strange sensation crept over Elizabeth, a picture of Kavan fresh in her mind.

❧

"Mom? Dad? Anybody here?" Elizabeth hollered a few hours later, walking through the front door of her parents' house. She tossed her overnight bag on the bottom step of the front staircase.

"Welcome home," her mother called, approaching from her office, arms wide.

"Hi, Mom." Elizabeth fell into her embrace and breathed in a scent like spring roses.

"Dinner's waiting in the oven. Your dad and Jonathan are washing up."

In the next instant, her brother bounded down the stairs and grabbed her in a big hug. "Lizbeth, you're home."

She laughed as he swung her around. "Put me down, you big lug."

"Good to see you, Kiddo." Her dad greeted her with a kiss.

"Good to be home, Daddy."

Dinner was a lively event with Chinese takeout. "I was too swamped at work this week to do the grocery shopping," Elizabeth's mom explained.

Her dad added, "We've been eating out every night, and it's costing us a fortune." He reached over to pinch his wife's cheek.

Jonathan regaled them with a lifeguard story from his summer job at the pool and announced to his sister his plans to be All-State after next year's football season.

Their father looked at him sideways, pointing his fork in Jonathan's direction. "Any plans to keep those grades up, Son?"

Elizabeth took a sip of water to hide her merriment. Her father's mock concern didn't fool her.

"Ah, Pop, Lizbeth is the brain in the family. I'm the brawn." He pushed up his shirtsleeve and flexed his muscles. Everyone laughed.

The conversation switched focus to Elizabeth when her dad asked, "How's grad school looking?"

Elizabeth felt like the sun had suddenly burned out. For a split second, she considered fabricating a story about her grad school status. But she knew it would be wrong and only prolong the agony of telling them the truth. "I've gotten two rejections."

"What?" they all said at once.

"Michigan and South Carolina."

Paul Lambert sat back in his chair, his hand propped on his leg. "Are you sure, Kiddo?"

"Hard to miss the word 'denied,' Dad. It's in black and white."

"Did you apply late?" Mom asked.

"Mom, please," Elizabeth replied.

"Well, of course not. I'm sorry, Elizabeth," her mother apologized.

A heavy silence hung over the dinner table. Elizabeth pushed the remains of an egg roll around on her plate. Finally she said, "There are three more schools. . . ."

"You'll get into one of them, surely." Vicki Lambert clicked her long fingernails and smiled. "God has a place for you."

The resounding ring of the phone pierced the gloom and sparked the family into motion. Jonathan bounded from the table like he was going for the goal line.

He smirked and handed the phone to Elizabeth. "It's for you."

She reached for the phone. "Hello."

A familiar squeal pierced her ear. "You're home! How long?"

Elizabeth smiled at the sound of her friend's voice. "Hi, Bailey. I'll be here until Wednesday."

"Let's do dinner."

Elizabeth agreed to meet Bailey and several other friends for dinner on Tuesday.

Later, in the kitchen, Elizabeth helped her dad clean up while her mother read to her from her electronic data assistant.

"You see Dr. Roth first thing in the morning. His office manager thinks they can get you new contacts by the late afternoon."

"Perfect!" Elizabeth stored the leftovers on the bottom shelf of the refrigerator.

"It was good of Conrad to squeeze you in." Dad rinsed the dishcloth, wrung out the excess water, and wiped down the table.

"I set you up with Dr. Geller on Tuesday for a dental cleaning," Mom said.

"Tuesday? How'd you get me in so fast?"

"Told them you were only home a few days."

Elizabeth shook her head. If anyone could work a deal, it was her mom. She bundled up a full trash bag and set it by the door to the garage. Behind her, Jonathan dropped a fresh bag into the kitchen garbage can.

"Don't forget to take out the trash, Son." Dad stood propped against the counter, legs crossed at the ankles, hands in his pockets. He regarded Elizabeth. "Grandpa tells me you have a *friend.*"

Elizabeth sat at the kitchen table with a cold diet soda and glass of ice. "Grandpa is practically delusional, Dad. You should really consider checking him into a padded room."

Jonathan laughed. "Not Grandpa. He's too cool."

"I don't see you having time for romance, Darling," Mom said, still focused on her electronic data assistant. Elizabeth glanced over to see her entering a list of to-dos.

"Exactly, Mom," she agreed. "I think all of White Birch has gone berserk with romantic notions. Every time I turn around, someone is trying to link me with Kavan Donovan.

"By the way, Dad, you never told me your family was so nosy."

Her mother laughed. "I told you, Paul."

"They aren't nosy, just interested, caring. . . ," he defended.

Elizabeth sipped her drink and sat cross-legged in the cushioned chair. "Don't get me wrong. I like White Birch. I'm actually having fun, which surprises me. But this whole 'get the granddaughter married off' has got to stop."

Her father walked over and kissed the top of her head.

"You'll be in grad school in less than two months. White Birch and all the talk of romance and Kavan will be a pleasant but fading memory."

Lying in her own bed that night, the silver moonlight illuminating her room, her dad's words echoed in her head. *A pleasant but fading memory.*

Tears stung in her eyes. She actually missed White Birch and Kavan. Did she really want it to end in two months?

She rolled over onto her side. Truth be told, Elizabeth didn't want Kavan Donovan to be a fading memory.

⁂

"Okay, Rick, stop. We'll unload the lumber here." Kavan unlatched the tailgate on his pickup and hopped into the bed. Rick joined him, hauling boards to the Division of Forests and Lands' Fourth of July exhibition site in the center of town.

Kavan paused to look around. The town square buzzed with holiday preparations. He rubbed his hands together and faced his lanky partner.

"Let's get this booth built," he said, pulling plans from his shirt pocket.

"What's Travis Knight on your case about?" Rick asked, taking the plans from Kavan.

"He claims my refurbishment budget for the White Birch tower is *way* overdrawn."

Rick shook his head. "Interesting."

"Yeah, I bought this stuff with my own money just to avoid the hassle."

"Doesn't seem right," Rick muttered.

"No, it doesn't." Kavan smoothed out the construction plans on the ground. "It's a simple frame booth, Rick."

For the next hour or so, the two worked on the fire safety booth for the Fourth of July celebration.

"Whatever happened to those poachers you chased down?" Rick asked, wiping the sweat from his brow with the back of his hand. "Never heard the end of that story."

"They got caught, did a few hours of community service."
Rick dropped his hammer in the toolbox. "They'll do it again."

"Or worse," Kavan concluded.

"Afternoon, gentlemen." Matt Lambert walked up to the display.

Rick and Kavan each shook his hand.

"Need some help? Woodworking is my specialty."

Kavan nodded in recognition. Indeed, Matt Lambert's craftsmanship bordered on legendary. "We're about done, Sir," he said. "Besides, we're just tapping together a few boards. Nothing fancy."

"Nevertheless, I should have strolled by sooner."

Kavan saw Rick peek at his watch. Dinnertime neared, and Rick had a new baby at home. "Why don't you go on, Rick. Grandpa Matt can help me finish up."

Rick thanked Kavan and dashed off toward his truck. Grandpa took up a hammer. "Elizabeth comes home tomorrow."

Kavan stretched the canvas across the back of the booth and grinned. "Is it tomorrow?"

"Yes, tomorrow." Grandpa tacked a nail into the canvas.

"Hmm," Kavan muttered.

Grandpa chuckled. "She won't be easy to catch, but it's possible."

Kavan moved to the side and held up the canvas. "Elizabeth doesn't want to be caught."

"Oh, she's caught all right," Grandpa said, nailing up the canvas for Kavan again. "She just doesn't know it."

Kavan shook his head. "I don't know, Grandpa."

Grandpa placed his hand on Kavan's shoulder. "Her whole life, she's set a goal and achieved it. Falling in love wasn't on the list. She's a lot like her sweet mother. Vicki is a very practical businesswoman. She wouldn't marry my son until he finished grad school and saved up several thousand dollars. That was a lot of money in the seventies."

Kavan gave a low whistle. He moved to the front of the

booth and covered the bottom half with more of the canvas.

Grandpa continued. "Elizabeth has this notion that falling in love is trivial, a waste of time. She's seen her friends lose focus on their careers and education because men tell them they are beautiful."

"Can't see Elizabeth doing that," Kavan said.

"No, she won't let herself."

Kavan stopped working and faced the older man. "Elizabeth has a lot of pride in her pursuits."

Grandpa nodded. "Won't deny it."

"I can't see her giving it all up for me or anyone."

"Maybe not now, but someday, my boy, someday. Be patient. Be her friend."

Kavan resumed work. "That's the plan, Gramps. That *is* the plan."

❧

On his back porch, Kavan sat in his rocker, gently swaying back and forth, the light of day evanescing. He sipped a cold bottle of soda and listened to the song of the breeze.

Talking to Grandpa Matt about Elizabeth stirred his longing for her. Though he confessed he would miss her, he'd tried to focus on other things while she was away.

Between his growing feelings for Elizabeth and the turmoil at work, Kavan made sure he took extra time each day to sit before the Father. Fortunately, Travis had taken the week off as vacation so the brewing trouble over the refurbishment budget was on the back burner.

Tipping his head back, Kavan took a deep breath. He loved the peaceful sounds of night and the abiding comfort of the Lord.

Now that his mind's eye was picturing the curly-haired brunette, he wanted to see her. He wondered what time she would be home and if he would see her soon. He imagined she'd have a full schedule between Lambert's Furniture and Sinclair's.

He reached for his cell phone. *Lord, should I call her?* He hesitated, punched in Elizabeth's cell number, but pressed the END button instead of TALK.

Grandpa Matt was right, he thought. *Elizabeth would be a hard one to catch.*

He punched in the number again and hit SEND before he could change his mind. He stood and leaned against the rail. *Friends, we're just friends.*

"Hello," she said, rather loud.

"Hi, it's Kavan." High-pitched voices and laughter filled his ear.

"Hello?" she repeated, louder.

"Elizabeth, it's Kavan."

"Just a second."

He could hear her shuffling around. The background noise faded.

"Wow, it's so noisy in the restaurant. I had to step outside."

He wanted to ask what she was doing, who she was with, but decided to keep his question neutral. "Having a good time?"

"Awesome." Her voice rose with excitement.

He smiled, picturing her face and the pink hue excitement always colored on her cheeks. "Sounds like a fun crowd."

"Bunch of engineering nerds." She laughed. "We've been talking shop."

Disappointment stabbed him, but he removed it from his voice when he said, "Good for you. Keep your eye on the goal."

"No doubt. These guys would never let me hear the end of it if I didn't go to grad school. Never."

"I'll let you go."

She suddenly asked, as if realizing Kavan Donovan was on the other end of the line, "Why did you call?"

"No reason."

"No reason?" She sounded suspicious.

"Yes. Drive home safe," he said, ready to hang up.

She snickered. "Is there any other way?"

"Guess not."

"Night, Kavan."

"Night, Elizabeth."

≈

On the Fourth of July, Elizabeth strolled the White Birch square with Ethan and Julie. While Ethan greeted practically everyone they passed, Julie and Elizabeth carried on an intimate discussion of graduate school.

"Don't get discouraged," Julie said. "You have the right stuff to get into the best schools. But, I remember the anxiety of waiting."

"Anxiety is putting it lightly," Elizabeth said with a chuckle. "It's just weird that I've been turned down and haven't heard from the remaining three schools."

"Come this way, ladies." Ethan motioned with his arm.

They followed. Julie gave a final word of advice. "If you don't hear from more schools, or if you get another rejection, call MIT's transcript office and have a copy of your transcript sent to you. It could have a clerical error."

Elizabeth opened her mouth in surprise. "I never thought of that."

Julie laughed. "You're a true linear thinking engineer, Beth. Gotta think outside the box sometimes."

Elizabeth spread out her arms and lifted her hands. "What can I say? Guilty as charged."

Laughing, they stopped beside Ethan and the fire safety booth. Kavan came around the corner with a passel of kids. He handed them balloons and candy, reminding them they could prevent forest fires.

"Hello." He glanced their way after sending the kids off.

"Nice display," Ethan commented as he scanned the booth.

Seeing Kavan made Elizabeth's heart dance, and she feared her feelings showed in her face. *Why does he affect me this way?*

"Hi, Elizabeth." He stepped toward her and kissed her cheek in greeting. "Welcome back."

"Good to be back," she said, his touch sparking a shiver.

Ethan started up a conversation, and the four of them chatted for a few minutes until another group of kids came strolling up, linked together by their hands. Some of them recognized Julie from school and called to her with a sweet chorus of "Hi, Mrs. Lambert."

While Julie hugged them and Ethan talked to more towns-folk, Elizabeth watched Kavan. He walked down the line of children, ruffling their hair, telling them they were going to learn how *not* to start a fire.

"Hey." He jogged over to her. "Want to help me with the kids?"

"Sure." For a split second, she was unable to imagine anything she'd want to do more.

"Great." He turned to walk away, hesitated, then faced her again. He pulled her into his embrace. "I'm really glad you're back."

She rested her head on his shoulder, breathing in the subtle scent of his cologne. "Me, too. Me, too."

eleven

As dusk settled over White Birch, Kavan put away the last of the coloring pens and construction paper. "Looks like everyone is settling in for dinner before the fireworks." He stepped around to the front of the booth and closed the distance between them.

Her eyes shimmered with excitement. "That was fun."

He smiled. "Yeah, the kids are great."

She stretched and then rested her hands in the hip pockets of her jean shorts. "What now?"

"Dinner. Everyone will picnic or go to one of the restaurants before the fireworks."

He watched Elizabeth survey the area. Large groups of people were already gathering by the lake, picking premium spots for the pyrotechnic show. Some stood eating hot dogs from street vendors; others unpacked picnic baskets.

"I'd better find Ethan and Julie."

Kavan reached for his toolbox. "Or," he started, "you can help me tear this down, and I'll treat you to pizza at Giuseppe's."

"Oh no, Kavan, you don't have to do that. I'll help, but you don't have to buy my dinner." She reached for a hammer.

"Consider it a payback. The kids loved you. Besides, before you left for Boston, we agreed to a pizza date."

Elizabeth stiffened. "Not a date. A, um, get-together."

He shook his head at her insistence. "You know, even friends can use the word "date." It doesn't have to imply anything romantic."

"Well, in this town, one cannot be too careful."

Grandpa Matt's words echoed through Kavan's head. *She won't be easy to catch, but it's possible.* Tearing apart the booth frame, Kavan wondered if he really wanted to catch Elizabeth

90

Lambert. There were a lot of other lovely and gracious women to choose from; he just. . .

He stopped in midthought. Who was he kidding? He had yet to meet a woman who captured his heart like Elizabeth had. Pride and all, he'd ask her to marry him in a heartbeat if he thought she'd say yes.

"What are you thinking about so intently, Donovan?" she asked, walking up behind him.

He turned toward her with a start. "Lost in thought."

She propped her hands on her hips. "I guess so. I called for you twice."

"Sorry, what did you need?"

"I folded the canvases and put them over there." She pointed to a spot beyond the booth. " 'Cause I didn't know where you parked your truck."

He faced the last two boards of the booth and hammered them apart. "The truck is down the street."

"I'm going to find Ethan and Julie so they know I'm having pizza with you. Do you want me to get your truck?"

"Yes, please." Kavan pulled his keys out of his pocket. Their fingers touched when he handed them to her. A tingle raced from the tip of his fingers to the top of his arm.

She glanced down at her hand holding the keys, then looked into his eyes. For a moment, he thought she was going to say she felt a tingle, too. "Wh–" She cleared her throat. "Where did you park the truck?"

He motioned over his shoulder. "On the other side of the post office."

He watched her hurry away.

Lord, if she's not the one for me, You'd better send a bolt of lightning. . . .

He gazed up at the twilight sky. *Not a cloud in sight.* He smiled.

❧

During dinner, Elizabeth studied him, trying to understand why the sound of his voice made her heart flip-flop. She focused on the strange feeling that came over her when she was in his presence, analyzing her thoughts and emotions. It couldn't merely be his striking face or lean, muscular frame. She knew lots of handsome men in college. In fact, one of her best buddies won a best-looking coeds contest. But Mark Wilder never made her feel the way Kavan Donovan made her feel.

During her short trip home to Boston, she renewed her commitment to grad school. How could she not complete the journey she'd begun?

Her mother's statement still echoed in her head. *I don't see you having time for romance, Darling.*

She's right, she's right. I don't have time for a serious relationship. School is my destiny. Elizabeth twirled the ends of her hair.

"I don't know what's going on with the budget," Elizabeth heard Kavan say as she brought her thoughts into the moment.

She propped her elbows on the table and gazed into his eyes. "I'm sorry, what? A budget?"

Kavan chuckled and fell back against his chair. "Earth to Elizabeth."

She grinned and hid her eyes behind her arm. "I'm sorry." She lowered her arm so she could see him and confessed, "Distracted by my own thoughts."

Kavan waved off her excuse. "I understand."

"So, tell me about this budget." Elizabeth picked up another slice of pizza. She took a bite and glanced at Kavan, waiting.

"Just boring work stuff." He took a drink from his soda.

"What's wrong with the budgets?"

"Not budgets. Bud*get*. Just one."

A flicker of concern reflected in his brown eyes, and compassion moved Elizabeth. She reached across the table and tapped his hand lightly. "Tell me what's wrong."

"Nothing's wrong, really." He shifted in his seat. "I am in charge of refurbishing the old White Birch fire tower, and it seems my budget is out of whack."

"What do you mean, 'out of whack'?" Elizabeth put her pizza slice down and pushed her plate away.

"Accounting claims I'm in the red, overdrawn. I can't seem to figure out what's going on. All they give us is a summary report."

She crossed her arms and leaned on the table. "Do you have records on your computer?"

He chewed a bite of pizza and nodded. The waitress came to the table and offered to refill their drinks.

"It's plugged into a spreadsheet. But the program I used for my spreadsheet keeps crashing. I can't get at the data. I have backups at home, but they're about a month behind. I've been too busy. . . ." He sighed and ran his hand across his forehead.

Elizabeth didn't know what to say, seeing his frustration and his uneasiness. "I'll pray for the Lord to bring you an answer."

He leaned forward. "Thank you. I appreciate it."

The subject changed, and by the time the waitress brought the bill, he had Elizabeth laughing over one of her cousin Jeff's high school antics.

She reached for the bill, but Kavan snatched the check out of her fingers. "Nothing doing. You helped me this afternoon, and I appreciate it."

She let the bill go. "Guess you can write it off as department expense."

Kavan feigned a laugh and pulled out his debit card. In a sardonic tone, he said, "I don't think so."

The waitress came over to pick up the bill with the card. Elizabeth excused herself to go to the ladies' room. She returned to the table just as Kavan signed the receipt.

"Ready?" he said, scribbling his name with a flourish.

Placing her hand on his shoulder, Elizabeth leaned over, squinting at the paper. "Again with that signature?" She laughed.

Kavan stood, a saucy grin on his lips. "I was premed for one quarter."

Elizabeth let go a robust chuckle and followed him to the door.

❧

"Your chariot, Milady." Kavan opened the truck door for Elizabeth, bowing low.

"Thank you, my lord." She hopped inside.

Kavan shut the door and walked around to the driver's side. He'd enjoyed dinner but felt like he spent too much time rehashing his work problems.

Ask Elizabeth about herself. He tried to think of something to ask her.

"I have a blanket in the back. Care to share it with me and watch the fireworks?" He started the engine with a quick turn of the ignition.

"Sounds like fun."

Kavan shifted the truck into gear and pulled out of the parking lot.

"Thanks for dinner," Elizabeth said softly.

He looked over at her. She was lovely to him, so very lovely. "Can't think of a better way to spend the Fourth of July."

They drove in silence to the lake. The quietness came with peace and comfort. Kavan held back from taking it as a sign of blessing from the Lord.

Parking close proved impossible, so Kavan found a spot at the end of Main Street. Casually, he slipped his hand into Elizabeth's as they walked toward the crowd.

"Any more news from grad schools?" he asked, determined to let her talk for awhile.

"No." Her voice rang flat in the night air.

"You will, don't worry."

"That's what I keep hearing."

He didn't miss the irritation in her voice.

"What's your focus again? Nuclear physics?"

"Engineering," she emphasized.

"Ah, right. Here's a spot over here."

She followed, but slipped her hand out of his. He glanced over his shoulder at her, gazing down on the top of her head. He couldn't see her face, but he sensed a change in her demeanor.

"What do you want to do with a master's in nuclear engineering?" He spread the blanket on the ground. "Here we go." He sat down, legs crossed at the ankle.

She stood, putting her hands on her hips. "What kind of question is that?"

He snapped his head up. Was she angry? In the fading light, he couldn't see her eyes. "What's the purpose of the degree? What field do you want to focus on? What kind of job are you thinking of getting?"

"Energy." She sat down on the edge of the blanket. "I'd like to work at a nuclear energy plant or do research."

"You've got to be kidding," he said. "Nuclear plants will be the death of us all if we don't—"

She cut him off. "Death of us all?"

"Ever hear of Chernobyl?" He fell back against the blanket, landing on his elbows.

"The safety of those reactors was ignored." Her voice warbled in a high pitch.

Across the lake, the first fireworks boomed and splashed fiery color in the night sky.

"Sure, and look at the devastation."

"You can't lump all nuclear reactors into the Chernobyl class. New energy standards are being generated every day."

"Yeah, like the standard of natural energy resources. We'd all be a lot better off—"

She hopped up again and peered down at him, hands on her hips. "Kavan, there are not enough natural resources to heat, cool, and feed the world. As it is now, most Third World countries are stripped of natural resources. Nuclear energy could provide relief for millions."

"And put them at risk." Kavan stood, not sure why he continued to banter with her. Clearly, the subject touched a nerve.

Another fireworks display exploded overhead. It popped open like an umbrella and sparks floated down. The crowd around them oohed and aahed.

She opened her arms. "Typical *naturalist*. The environment is all you care about. Yet you want to deprive millions the luxury of affordable energy. Meanwhile, the earth is drained of natural resources. All the while, your crowd insists nuclear energy will be the death of us all. You can't have it both ways, Kavan."

What is she saying? He reached for her arm and asked in a low tone. "Elizabeth, are you sure you're still talking about energy resources?"

Boom! Phosphorus light splashed against the darkness, and for a split second, he could see the hard lines drawn on her face.

"What else would I be talking about?" she snapped, turning on her heel. "I'll see you later, Kavan. Julie and Ethan are probably wondering where I am." She walked away, and in only a few steps, Kavan lost sight of her in the crowd and shadows.

twelve

Elizabeth rode in silence to Grandpa and Grandma's house in the backseat of Ethan and Julie's car. She listened to their intimate conversation about the day's events that touched them. Julie enjoyed seeing the children and the fireworks, and Ethan rather liked socializing with White Birch's citizens.

"What'd you like most about the day?" Julie asked, adjusting to face Elizabeth. The lights from the dash showed her pretty smile.

Elizabeth gave a generic, safe answer. "The fireworks."

What she wanted to say was the entire day: Kavan and the fire safety booth, Kavan and dinner, Kavan and the fireworks. Yet, the entire situation conflicted her. How could she have feelings for him? Emotional attachments could devastate her future plans.

When he asked her about school, panic gripped her. She had not thought about higher education since she laid eyes on him at the fire safety booth. Not once!

She was going to let her dream go all because she allowed a summer crush to weave its way into her heart. So, she picked a fight. Thinking about it now, she felt guilty. But she had to get away from him, put some distance between them.

She sighed and dropped her head against the window. *My friends would never let me hear the end of it. I gave them such a hard time when each of them fell in love.*

Suddenly, she sat up straight and stared out the front window. She clenched her jaw in resolution. *I won't lose sight of school. I won't fall for Kavan.*

Ethan turned into the driveway and started up the hill toward the house.

"Thanks for the ride home." Elizabeth leaned forward

97

between the front seats.

Ethan smiled at her. "We had fun. Thanks for hanging with us."

Julie objected with a wink. "I think she spent more time with a handsome ranger than us, Babe."

Ethan chuckled as he pulled around by the kitchen door. Elizabeth fell back against her seat. "He's a friend, you two. A *friend*."

"They make the best partners." Julie glanced over her shoulder at her cousin-in-law.

Elizabeth stared straight into her eyes. "I'm going to grad school."

"I married Ethan right out of high school, and I still earned my master's." Julie's statement caused another wave of panic to splash over Elizabeth.

"Good for you." She reached for the door handle. "Marriage is not for me."

"Will it ever be?" Julie asked.

Elizabeth yanked the handle and opened the door slightly. "What is with this family and marriage?"

"We find it rather pleasant, and safe, and wonderful," Julie said.

Ethan added, "Beth, marriage isn't the issue; your ardent opposition to marriage is the issue."

"Oh, right, Ethan. I'm the bad guy 'cause I'd rather finish school than be a giggly, lovesick house Frau." She shoved the door the rest of the way open and stepped out. Her irritation showed and she knew it. "I'm sorry, you guys, I'm tired."

"Don't worry about it, Beth," Julie said. "Call me later if you need to talk."

"Thanks. Good night." Elizabeth watched them drive away, and instead of going inside, she slipped down the side of the hill toward the covered bridge. Her emotions felt raw and exposed. As she moved under the cover of the bridge, tears spilled down her cheeks. She fought for control.

"Lord, I know I haven't been close to You lately, but since

You are my Friend, can I talk to You?" More tears came. For the longest time, Elizabeth walked the length of the bridge, unburdening her heart to the Lord. No cars drove past, and it seemed that the Lord arranged a private audience just for her, His friend.

&

Kavan woke feeling as if he'd never been asleep. He slapped the snooze button on his alarm and buried his head under the pillow. He'd tossed and turned most of the night, his dreams invaded by fireworks and Elizabeth's sharp, sarcastic words, followed by Travis Knight's accusations and mistrust.

Last night, he sat on the porch, praying until midnight, asking the Lord to search him. The recent refurbishment fiasco and Travis's subtle imputations, coupled with Elizabeth's erratic behavior, caused him to wonder if the Lord was trying to tell him something.

He dozed for a few more minutes before the alarm sounded a second time. He sat up slowly and dangled his legs over the side of the bed. With a yawn, he headed for the shower. Morning light filtered through the bathroom window. Kavan hovered over the sink, splashing his face with cold water. *Gotta wake up.*

He brushed his teeth, shaved, and showered. Dressed in a freshly laundered uniform, he headed to the kitchen to make some coffee. Fred and Ginger waited by the back door, tails wagging.

"Morning, Fred. Morning, Ginger." He stroked them each on the head before turning the knob. They bolted out into the fresh morning air. Kavan left the door ajar and popped a couple pieces of bread into the toaster. When the coffee finished brewing, he poured a cup and took it to the porch along with the toast.

Sipping his coffee and munching his breakfast, he meditated on the Lord. A verse from the book of Psalms flowed through his head. *Search me, O God. . .test me. . . See if there is any offensive way in me.*

Nothing came to mind. "Lord, I trust You to take care of me. My reputation is in Your hands. You will accomplish what concerns me."

He went inside after a few more minutes and set his dishes in the sink. He picked up the floppy with the refurbishment data on it and headed for work. First thing on his morning agenda was to get his office computer installed with a new spreadsheet program and load his backup records. With Travis on vacation, he had time to figure out what was going on.

"Morning, Rick." Kavan walked over to his desk.

Rick looked up. "Oh—um, Kavan. Good morning."

Kavan furrowed his brow and gave his coworker a second glance. He pulled up to his desk and booted up the computer. Reaching in his top desk drawer, Kavan retrieved the new software CD. "You okay, Rick?"

"Sure. Fine." He smiled. "Seems the fire safety booth was a success."

Kavan nodded. "The kids loved it. And. . ." He leaned back and arched his brow at Rick. "I had the prettiest assistant in White Birch."

Rick chuckled and consented with a nod. "Anything going on between you two?"

He didn't mean to, but Kavan sighed. "Just friends."

⁂

On his way home that night, Kavan took a detour to the fire tower. He wanted to resume the refurbishment project, but as long as the matter of the budget remained unresolved, he felt shackled. Climbing the old stairs to the top, Kavan gazed out over the White Mountains. He took the steps near the top two at a time.

He pushed open the trapdoor of the tower floor and climbed inside. He leaned out the tower window, and with a loud voice he hollered, "Good evening, Lord. Evening, White Mountains."

He closed his eyes and breathed in the night mountain air. *Fresh and clean. . .* He stopped. His eyes popped open and scanned the horizon. Kavan took another deep breath.

He smelled smoke.

In one quick motion, he found the tower's stored binoculars and lifted them to his eyes. To the west, along the ridge, dark smoke billowed above the trees.

His heartbeat quickened.

Fire!

❧

Closing the kitchen door, Elizabeth turned and kissed Grandma on the cheek, then snatched a warm cookie from the cooling rack.

"How was your day?" Grandma asked.

"Wonderful." Elizabeth dashed to the stairs. "Gotta change for Sinclair's. Be down in a minute."

She hummed as she changed her clothes and wrapped her long curls into a ponytail. She grabbed a makeup brush and touched up her foundation and cheek color before heading back downstairs.

Since her unburdening with Jesus last night, she felt renewed. If coming to White Birch for the summer produced nothing more than reconnecting with her friend Jesus, it was well worth it. She regretted her time in college where she dismissed the tugging of the Holy Spirit on her heart. She wouldn't make the same mistake in graduate school.

In the kitchen, Grandpa sat at the table with a stack of cookies and a tall glass of milk in front of him. He reached for the first cookie from the stack.

Elizabeth stopped and stared at him. "You can't be serious."

"I am." He winked at his wife.

"Your cholesterol must be ridiculous."

Grandma waved her spatula in the air. "He's healthier than men half his age. Got a hollow leg, that one. Never could seem to fill him up."

Elizabeth opened the fridge door and pulled out a packet of turkey and a slice of cheese. Grabbing the mayonnaise and mustard, she went to the counter to make a sandwich.

"While you're making that sandwich, Bethy, mind if I talk

to you?" Grandpa asked. He picked up another cookie.

"Sure, Grandpa." Elizabeth peeked at him over her shoulder. She took two pieces of bread from the wrapper and set them on a paper towel.

"I got some of those lunch-size chips for you today," Grandma interjected. "They're in the pantry."

"Yum. . . Thanks, Grandma."

"I want to talk about grad-u-ate school." He reclined comfortably in his chair at the kitchen table.

Elizabeth laughed at his inflection. "What about grad-u-ate school?"

"Why are you going?"

A cold chill ran down her spine. At the same time, she felt a hot flash burn her cheeks. *He sounds like Kavan.*

"It's my destiny, Grandpa. You know that. Dad, Mom, and I have talked about it since I was twelve."

Grandpa motioned for her to sit by him. Grandma finished making her sandwich.

"I've been praying for you, Bethy. I'm not sure this is the time for you to go to graduate school. You have a fine degree in electrical engineering. I happen to know that Creager Electronics is hiring electrical engineers."

Why is he bringing this up? Her insides trembled as if she were cold. "Don't tell me you pulled a string for me at Creager, Grandpa. I'm going to grad school."

"Did you know I went to Harvard after the war?"

Elizabeth's eyes widened. "Harvard? No, you didn't."

"I did." Grandpa confirmed with a slight nod, picking up a third cookie.

"You are full of surprises." Elizabeth smiled.

"But you know, Bethy, I had no business being at Harvard. I didn't have any scholarly interest. I was just doing it because my pride wanted a Harvard diploma hanging on my wall. After all, I'd been to war. I was a man." Grandpa tapped his fist on his chest. "But deep down I knew I wanted to take over your great-grandpa's business here in White Birch."

Grandma said in a small voice, "My father promised us his mill business, which your grandpa grew into Lambert's Furniture."

Elizabeth turned to her grandpa. "What happened?"

He swallowed a bite of cookie, gazed toward his wife, and recounted. "We had no car, very little money. One snowy morning, I skipped classes, pretending to be sick. I told Betty I'd study at home." He paused, shifting his gaze to Elizabeth.

"Your grandma was pregnant with your aunt Barbara and had to go to work while I slept until noon. That evening I looked out the window to see my pregnant wife walking home from work in the falling snow, carrying a sack of groceries. She slipped on the ice and nearly fell. A passerby caught her arm and steadied her."

"How come I never heard this story before?" Elizabeth wanted to know. She glanced from her grandpa to her grandma and back again.

Grandpa shrugged and finished his story. "That night, the Lord spoke to me out of I Peter, 5." Grandpa quoted the verse. " 'Young men, in the same way be submissive to those who are older. All of you, clothe yourselves with humility toward one another, because, "God opposes the proud but gives grace to the humble." ' "

A flush warmed Elizabeth's neck and face. "What's your point, Grandpa?" She peeked at her watch.

"I love you, Beth. But I believe your pride is causing you to pursue the advanced degree. Do you really want to study nuclear engineering?"

She pushed back her chair and stood. "It's a prestigious, lucrative field, Grandpa. And it's very open to women."

"Electrical engineering is a lucrative career, too. Also, open to women."

"I'm going to grad school," Elizabeth said between clenched teeth.

"You sound like me sixty years ago when I wanted to go to Harvard. No advice of my father's or Betty's would change my mind. Then I see my wife, carrying my child, working harder than I was at keeping us together." Grandpa bowed his head and softened his voice. "It humbles me still."

Elizabeth rested her hands on the back of the chair. "You make my point. That's why I'm not about to get into a relationship until I'm finished with school."

"Wise decision," Grandpa countered. "However, my challenge to you, Beth, is not about Kavan or marriage, but your purpose in going to grad school. Pray; ask the Lord to reveal the secrets of your heart."

Elizabeth regarded him without saying a word. She loved and respected him too much to ignore his words. "I have to go to work."

"Pray about what I said," Grandpa said.

She grabbed her purse and started for the door. "I'll pray, but I promise you, I'm going to grad school."

❧

On the drive to Sinclair's, Elizabeth replayed the kitchen conversation, churning over Grandpa's words, searching for any truth to his challenge.

"Lord, is he right? I've planned on going to grad school for so long, I can't imagine *not* going. Everyone expects me to go. Mom, Dad, and Jonathan. . .my friends. But what is Your plan for my life?"

Before she resolved the issue in her mind and with the Lord, she arrived at Sinclair's. Elizabeth zipped into the large parking lot and dashed inside.

"Sorry I'm late, Joann."

Her boss followed her to the time clock. "No problem. Just relieve Molly at the service desk. Everything okay?"

Elizabeth paused, then looked her boss in the eyes. "I'm not sure. Grandpa thinks I don't really know why I'm going to grad school. That I have no purpose for going."

"Ha, I've been saying that since the moment I met you."

Elizabeth held up her hand and rolled her eyes. "Don't start."

She headed toward the front counter. Joann followed,

reminding her to count down the afternoon tills and refill the candy racks by the cash register. Suddenly a blaring siren filled Elizabeth's ears. "What *is* that?" she asked, halting in the middle of the aisle.

Concern covered Joann's face. "Fire siren, calling all the volunteers."

Several men rushed past them out of the store.

From her post at the service desk, Elizabeth watched as men and women rushed in and out. Finally, she asked one of them, "Where is the fire?"

"Up on Pine Knoll Mountain. The rangers are fighting it now, but volunteers are being called in." He paid for his purchase and hurried away.

Kavan!

Throughout the night, news trickled into the store about the fire. Many believed it had been contained, but none of the rangers or volunteer firefighters had emerged.

Elizabeth could not stop thinking about Kavan. She called his house and cell phone. No answer. She prayed for the Lord to protect him, but her heartbeat pounded with concern for him like the ticking of the clock.

"Go," Joann finally said an hour before Elizabeth's shift ended.

"Go?"

"Go to the command center. See if he's okay."

Elizabeth hustled around the counter and darted toward the time clock.

"Keep me posted," Joann called after her.

"I will. I will."

She ran to clock out and grab her backpack.

&

Somehow, in the chaos, she found Jeff. With his help, Elizabeth made her way to the fire's command center. She parked her VW out of the way and stood on the perimeter of the activity. In the distance, she could see the fire burning along the ridge, trees flaming like matchsticks.

The mountainside was engulfed in flames. Fire billowed up from the surface and danced across the treetops.

"Kavan!" a uniformed ranger communicated with the fire-fighters over a large, handheld radio.

From her vantage point, Elizabeth tried to spot Kavan among the men at the command center, hoping to see him safe in the crowd. But there was no sign of him. *He's on that ridge; I just know it.* Her heart hurt with anxiety.

thirteen

Kavan trailed the firefighters working along the ridge, flanking the fading fire, beating out hot spots. A chain saw dangled from one hand. He anchored a pickax with the other. Grateful for the cool night air and the valiant efforts of the firefighters, he believed the blaze to be contained. The knot in his stomach loosened slightly.

The radio strapped to his side crackled and clicked. Kavan tilted his ear toward the sound. "The wind is picking up, Kavan," the operations officer, Steve Mayer, warned over the radio.

Kavan peered over his shoulder, scanning the area he and the other firefighters had just covered. From the service road where they'd been dropped off to the point where they now stood, the embers burned low. "Steve, what does it look like from down there?"

"Fire is burning along the bottom of the ridge, but it's dying down."

"We're still fighting hot spots," Kavan reported.

"Watch the wind," Steve warned again.

The knot in Kavan's middle tightened. "Copy. I'll keep an eye out. Over."

The radio fell silent. Kavan hiked up the ridge, picking at hot spots, watching the progress of the other eight firefighters as they climbed higher. He could feel the wind gusting through the trees.

"Lord, calm the wind." He watched Rick beat out another burning patch.

Ash fluttered in the air, and the smell of smoke permeated Kavan's nostrils. The wind knocked against him.

Up ahead, hot spots still ignited. Behind him, the burned area smoldered with dying embers. So far there existed no threat of the fire igniting again. Vigilant, Kavan stepped forward.

"What's the word, Kavan?" Chet, one of the firefighters asked, pausing to wait for his leader.

"Strong wind gust. Stay alert."

The firefighter nodded and went back to work. Several of the others beat out a spot fire.

Kavan worked the draw between the two ridges, climbing upward while swinging his pickax. The labor made the muscles in his shoulders ache, and the knee he'd injured chasing the poachers throbbed with pain.

More than seven hours had passed since he'd first spotted the smoke. He and his crew had worked tirelessly since the initial fire siren, breaking briefly just after dark to eat and rest. Kavan aimed his flashlight at his watch.

Midnight.

A picture of Elizabeth flashed through his weary thoughts. It seemed like forever since he'd seen her.

Kavan peered over his shoulder again, down the ridge. The smell of smoke intensified. Embers floated in the wind, and it alarmed him. Kavan made a quick assessment of the area, plotting an escape route, just in case those embers landed on fresh kindling. The men on the ridge were in his charge.

In the next minute, Steve called over the radio. "Team three, be advised the wind is picking up. Teams one and two are coming in. Over."

Kavan didn't like the eerie feel of the wind, either. "Ten-four. Send the pickup. We'll work our way down to the service road. Over."

"Truck is on its way. Over."

Relief popped inside of him when Steve radioed that the truck was on its way. Kavan instructed his team to sweep the area and head for the pick-up location.

The firefighters beat out hot spots while traversing toward the meeting point. Kavan's stomach rumbled with hunger. One of the men told a joke and had them all laughing just as Steve radioed again.

"Team three! Kavan!" Steve sounded panicked. "The access road is blocked. The wind ignited the fire. It's jumped to the trees. Get out of there! Over."

Kavan whipped around and ran to the top of the crevasse. The orange glow of fire and swirling smoke filled the horizon. Wind gusts funneled up the ridge. It was only a matter of time before the entire area would be consumed by fire.

"Crown fire! Run!" Kavan shouted, adrenaline driving him toward the top of the ridge.

❧

Elizabeth hustled with the other volunteers at the command post, serving sandwiches and water to tired firefighters. A friend of her grandmother's had spotted her and enlisted her aid. Elizabeth welcomed the distraction. Concern for Kavan had her insides twisted into nervous knots.

She watched the men in charge from the edge of activity, listening as the man referred to as the operations officer directed the fire-fighting teams.

She lifted her head when she heard him bellow Kavan's name into the small black radio. Her heartbeat seemed to stop for a moment. Making herself small, she inched along the perimeter of the command post, yearning to hear more.

"Kavan, are you there?"

Elizabeth waited for the buzz of Kavan's voice over the radio, but no response came.

"Team three, come in! Kavan," the man shouted.

When the radio remained silent, she heard him whisper, "Come on, Man, where are you?"

Elizabeth's knees buckled, but she caught herself. *Kavan, oh, Kavan, be all right. Please! Jesus, Jesus. . .*

The hair on her arms stood up, and a prickly feeling ran down her back.

"Get the helicopter up," the commander ordered.

Yes, do that, Elizabeth thought. *Find them. Please.*

She closed her eyes to pray, but a jolt caused her to open

them. The operations officer stood before her.

"Can I help you?"

She swallowed and said in a shallow tone, "I'm a volunteer and, um, a friend of Kavan Donovan's."

He looked into her eyes. "He'll be all right. Smart one, that Kavan."

"Yes, I know." She slipped back into the shadows, using every ounce of faith to fuel the power of her prayers. "Jesus, my Friend, hear my prayer. Protect Your friends up on that ridge. Kavan loves You. Let him know You are with him now. You are good, and I trust You."

Hours passed. Elizabeth continued to pray as she worked along with the other volunteers. She could hear the dialogue between the man who spoke to her and the helicopter pilot.

"Any sign of them? Over."

"None," the pilot answered.

Glancing overhead, Elizabeth watched the helicopter circle the ridge, the enormous spotlight floating over the fading flames as two other teams fought the fire.

"Scan the bottom of the ridge. Surely they ran down the other side."

"Ten-four."

Biting the inside of her lip, Elizabeth strained to hear the pilot's response. It felt like an eternity passed before he came back over the radio.

"No sign."

When the commander sighed and dropped his head, despair snapped at Elizabeth. Tears blurred her vision. She remembered stories about wildfires and how their intense heat and fast-moving blaze could easily overtake a man.

From behind, a strong hand gripped her shoulders. "How are you holding up?" a familiar voice asked.

Elizabeth turned to meet the tender expression of her grandpa. "Not sure. Oh, Grandpa. . ." Her voice broke.

Grandpa embraced her. "The Lord knows what's going on. Let's keep praying. I believe it's going to be okay."

Elizabeth rested her head on his shoulder and prayed with him in silent unison. Finally, she stepped back and took a deep breath, smoothing her curls. Weary, but peaceful, she wondered aloud, "What time is it?"

"A little after midnight."

Gazing toward the ridge, she said, "He has to be okay, Grandpa. He has to be."

❧

Kavan's chest burned from breathing smoke as he ran uphill. His weak knee buckled several times when his foot landed on uneven terrain. Rick, Chet, and the other firefighters fell in behind him, single file. They could now see the glow of the fire a couple hundred yards behind them. The flames chased them up the hill. Treetops exploded into balls of fire.

Kavan reached for his radio, but it was not there. "I lost my radio," he shouted over his shoulder.

"Where are we going?" Rick asked, running on Kavan's flank.

"A cave!" Kavan directed.

Rick nodded.

Kavan led the troop several yards before the opening to the cave came into view. In one accord, the firefighters sprinted to safety as hot embers began to rain down on them. Inside the cave, they fell against the stone walls. Kavan tugged off his headgear and turned his face into a cool draft.

"There's an opening at the back of the cave. The draw from the fire is creating a breeze," he said, turning to Rick and the rest of the team. He smiled.

The others removed their headgear; laughter of relief echoed throughout the cave. Firefighter Liam Watson clicked on his lamp. The single glow filled the cave with low light.

The knot in Kavan's middle unraveled. With a quick scan, he counted to make sure each man had arrived to safety. *All here. Thank You, Lord.* He sighed a prayer.

"You did a good job out there," he said, letting his gaze fall on each man.

"We owe you," Liam said. "You were the only one who

knew about this cave. We'd still be running."

A thin laugh escaped Kavan's lips. "I explored this cave as a kid. But I gotta tell you, I wasn't sure this was the right ridge." His body trembled as his nerves unwound and his taut emotions drained. "Rick, do you still have your radio?"

"Yeah." Rick clicked it on and tried to contact the command post. "Cave is blocking the signal."

Kavan dropped some of his gear to the cave floor and slid down against the rugged cave wall, favoring his bum knee. "When the fire burns through, we'll go back down the ridge through the burn area. Until then, have a seat."

The clamor of equipment releasing and hitting the ground echoed throughout the cave. No one spoke, each man left to his own reflection. Kavan used the last of his energy to pray. *Thank You, Lord, for hiding us in the cleft of this rock. Thank You.*

He closed his eyes and dreamt of Elizabeth.

☙

Exhausted, Elizabeth contemplated going home. But how could she when Kavan remained in harm's way? Grandpa had bid her good night a half hour ago, but he didn't try to convince her to leave.

I have to know he's all right.

With the blaze fading and contained, most of the volunteers had gone home. Wives of the firefighters remained, serving sandwiches and drinks to the returning teams. Blackened by smoke and exhausted, the firefighters collapsed on the ground around the command center. Silence hovered over them and, to Elizabeth, the ever-present knowledge that nine men had not returned.

"Lord, I know You are with them," she prayed, understanding that the peace she experienced was God's touch on her heart.

Suddenly, a strong, moist wind whipped through the camp, then a sweet, drizzling rain began to fall. Cheers erupted around the command center. Elizabeth joined them, laughing, clapping, cheering.

The operations officer shouted into the jubilation, "Team

three is safe. They're on their way to the access road."

Elizabeth trembled with relief, and tears pooled in her eyes. "Thank You, Jesus. Thank You."

❧

In the distance, she watched the all-terrain vehicle bounce over charred ground toward them.

Kavan's safe. I can go home now, she resolved. But her feet refused to move. She stood planted by the food table, her gaze fixed in the distance. A load of soot-covered firefighters piled out of the all-terrain vehicle and walked toward the command center.

Amid cheering and applause, the firefighters entered the command center. With so many voices talking at once, Elizabeth could hardly make out the story they were trying to tell. Her gaze fell on Kavan. He looked absolutely wonderful, grime and all.

He dropped his gear to the ground and left the others for a drink of water. He downed a large bottle of water, then he spotted her. His gaze, intense and steady, locked onto hers. He set his water bottle on the table and strode toward her.

Trembling and overwhelmed, she started to cry.

Without a word, Kavan drew her to him. She lifted her face to his just as he bent toward her. With tender passion, his lips covered hers.

fourteen

Kavan woke late Wednesday morning. He was beginning to feel like his old self, having slept most of Tuesday and late this morning. He moved about slowly, feeling the ache in his knee as he showered and dressed, then tended the dogs. He decided to head into town for breakfast at the diner. He didn't have to work, and a late breakfast sounded just like what the doctor ordered.

He pulled into a slanted parking space along Main Street and shut off the truck engine.

"Welcome, Kavan, welcome!" the diner's proprietor, Sam Whitfield, greeted him, shuffling out from behind the counter. "Take this booth by the window. Best seat in the house."

Kavan stared at Sam, puzzled by his curious behavior. "Thanks, Sam." He slid into the booth.

"What'll ya have? It's on the house." The older gentleman hovered over him, exposing his big teeth.

"On the house?"

"On the house," Sam repeated.

"What for?"

"Ain't you seen the paper? You're a hero. Saved those boys up on the ridge."

Kavan stood, crashing his legs into the booth table. "What?"

"Maybel, bring Kavan some coffee and the morning paper."

Kavan eased back down into the booth seat.

"What'll you have, Kavan?"

He hesitated. *Hero?*

"Kavan?" Sam tapped his pen against the table.

Snapping to attention, Kavan answered, "The day's special with a side of pancakes."

"Coming up. Coming right up." Sam sauntered back to the kitchen.

Maybel brought the paper and poured coffee. "Nice picture of you," she said.

There on the front page of the *White Birch Record* was a picture of him and the eight men of team three. The headline read, "Ranger Kavan Donovan leads firefighters to safety."

"Nice work up there, Donovan," a diner patron commented on his way out.

Kavan looked up. Unsure of what else to say, he answered, "Thank you."

Other townsfolk stopped by his table, congratulating him and calling him a hero. He squirmed with embarrassment. When Sam brought his food, Kavan welcomed the distraction.

"Lord, what's going on?" he whispered in prayer, his head bowed over his plate.

I honor those who honor Me. The subtle impression surprised Kavan, but he could tell by the impact the words had on his heart that the Living Lord had just touched him.

Finishing his breakfast, he downed the last of his coffee. His cell phone rang.

"Good job up on that ridge, Donovan."

"Thank you, Travis." Kavan reclined against the back of the booth, dubious. "How was your vacation?"

"Too much family. I'm glad to be home."

Kavan smiled.

"Seems the town fathers want to honor you and the others in a little ceremony."

Kavan winced. "You don't say?" He didn't understand the big to-do. "We were just doing our job."

"Well, the townspeople just want to say thanks."

Rubbing his forehead with his fingers, Kavan asked, "When?"

"Friday night. Eight o'clock at the civic center."

"I'll be there."

"Kavan, don't think this gets you off the hook on your budget discrepancies."

He sighed. "I'll be in the office tomorrow."

Kavan went up to the counter to pay for breakfast.

"No siree, it's on the house." Sam pushed the money in Kavan's hand away.

"No, Sam, let me pay."

"Heroes eat for free in my place." He flashed his toothy grin. "Haven't had a hero around here in awhile."

None of Kavan's arguments could convince him otherwise. He stepped outside into the warm July sun. Passersby honked and waved, calling out to him. He felt like Rip van Winkle. The world had drastically changed while he'd slept for two days.

Cruising slowly down Main Street, Kavan gathered his thoughts. Then, as if all the forces in his brain converged at once, he remembered! *I kissed Elizabeth.*

His heartbeat quickened with the memory of their first kiss. He glanced at his watch. He'd barely talked to her since that intimate moment. Right after the kiss, he had been called away to report on the fire to the operations officer. By the time he finished, she had disappeared.

Turning right at the next street, Kavan headed for Lambert's Furniture.

As his thoughts cleared, the postfire events flashed through his mind. He'd crawled into bed sometime early Tuesday, and except for a brief lunch Tuesday afternoon, he'd been sleeping ever since.

I've got to talk to her!

❧

"Hey, Elizabeth," Kavan said, peering around her office door.

She jumped to her feet. Papers fluttered to the floor. "Kavan."

"You got a minute?" Kavan stepped through the doorway.

Anticipation prevented her from speaking, so she simply pointed to the chair opposite her desk.

"I was wondering," he said slowly as he eased into the chair, his gaze fixed on her, "if you wanted to go for a cup of coffee or something."

She nodded, then managed an answer. "I was about to go to lunch."

"I just had breakfast, but do you mind if I tag along?"

Again, she nodded a response, unsure of her speech. Reaching for her purse, she glanced at Kavan and asked, "The diner okay?"

He grinned. "I'd rather avoid the diner if you don't mind. Giuseppe's?"

She relaxed and smiled. "Sounds good to me. I could eat their pizza every day."

They drove to Giuseppe's in Kavan's truck. He appeared to be deep in thought, so she rode quietly beside him. She wasn't too sure what to say anyway. "Why did you kiss me?" felt like an awkward way to start a conversation.

Kavan pulled into Giuseppe's lot and parked. His hand paused on the keys as he cut the engine, then he turned toward her and said, "I kissed you."

His pointed statement pierced the tension, and Elizabeth laughed out loud. "I know."

He chuckled. "The entire drive over here, I wondered how to bring it up, then bam, it just came out."

"I wondered how to bring it up, as well," she confessed. She loved his honesty and the sure way he regarded her.

He slid across the bench seat to grab her hand. "I'm sorry I didn't call you. I slept almost nonstop once I got home, and it wasn't until I finished breakfast this morning that I remembered what happened."

She broke her gaze and stared down at her fingers. "I understand."

He lifted her chin with the tender touch of his fingers and peered into her eyes. "Do you?"

She looked away. "Yes." How could she tell him?

"Elizabeth, what's wrong?" Kavan insisted. "I hope I didn't offend you by kissing you. It's just, well, when I saw you standing there. . . You were the last person I expected to see. Guess my heart overtook my head."

Tears slipped from her eyes. "I was so happy to see you walking out of that fire alive."

He chuckled. "I was happy to be walking out of the fire."

"I wanted to run up to you, but I couldn't." She wiped away the tears.

He waited, listening, smoothing her hair with his hand. She loved his touch. *Say it out loud, Elizabeth.*

"That was my first kiss." *There, I said it.*

His eyes popped wide open. "Ever?"

She laughed through the returning tears. "Well, since Jude McAllister kissed me in fourth grade on a dollar dare."

They stared at each other for a moment, then filled the cab of the truck with simultaneous laughter. "A dollar dare, huh?" Kavan repeated.

"Yep."

"Who made the dare?"

"Me!" Elizabeth pointed toward herself with her thumb. "I wanted to buy an ice cream bar and a soda after school."

Their laughter rose again. "My mother quickly gave me a lesson about girls who kiss for money."

Kavan guffawed and slapped his knee. "I can't picture it. I can't picture it."

She liked to hear him laugh. It made her feel light and free. Suddenly, he grew serious. "I meant that kiss, Elizabeth."

Her insides quivered. "So did I."

&

"So," Grandpa said after dinner, "I hear you ate at Giuseppe's this afternoon with our local hero."

Elizabeth set down the glass she pulled from the cupboard. "Is nothing sacred in this town?"

Grandpa looked up and rubbed his chin. "No, don't reckon so. Especially a pizza date."

"Date. . .it was lunch!"

"You thought any more about what I told you?"

"A little." She poured a glass of diet soda and joined Grandpa at the table.

"And?"

"Kavan is wonderful. Funny how it took the fire to make me realize how much I care for him. But, Grandpa, this finding doesn't preclude my plans. I can't fall in love. Not now."

"Your pride is tougher than I thought. I'm going to double my prayers."

"You amaze me, you know that?"

Grandma entered the kitchen. "Bethy, I forgot to tell you. More university letters came today."

Elizabeth jumped up. She'd sat down to dinner right after work without bothering to go upstairs. "Thick or thin?"

"Thin."

Elizabeth dashed upstairs, struggling under the weight of looming disappointment.

In her room, she flipped on a light and booted her laptop. Sure enough, two thin letters sat on the desk. She sank onto the bed reading the first rejection letter, then the next.

She stared blankly, letting the letters slip from her fingers to the floor.

Lord, I don't understand. I don't understand. Elizabeth's confusion bubbled into frustration spiked with a little anger. She hopped off the bed and paced the room.

This is ridiculous. And not my plan! She moaned and covered her face with her hands. How could this be happening to her? She thought for a moment, deciding to check her E-mail. Perhaps she would discover a clue to this whole mystery.

A half dozen new E-mails displayed in the inbox. Two were from Jenna, asking if she had been accepted at Ohio State. She really wanted to room with Elizabeth.

Elizabeth clicked the REPLY button, started to type, and then cleared the message. *I can't tell her the truth, yet.*

The rest of the E-mails were from family—her mom and brother. He wrote more about his summer antics at the public swimming pool. She smiled. Jonathan had a way about him that deflected her frustrations. Kavan, she was discovering, had the same effect on her.

She started to reply to her brother, but a subtle nudge prompted her to respond to Jenna.

Humble yourself, Elizabeth. She squirmed, remembering her haughty attitude toward the family about her educational pursuits. Highlighting Jenna's E-mail, Elizabeth clicked the REPLY button. Fingers poised on the keys, she pondered what to say and how.

She whispered, "Lord, what should I say?"

The truth.

Elizabeth sighed. "The truth, eh?"

"Hi, Jenna," she typed, and the rest of the message flowed from her fingertips. A page or so later, Elizabeth typed her name and clicked SEND.

A nervous flutter caused doubt to rise, but only for a moment. After that, a confidence came, and Elizabeth knew her friend Jesus would handle the rest.

"Scary place to be, Lord, but I trust You."

Just then, Grandma called up the stairs. "Your grandpa and I are going out for ice cream. Since you're not working at Sinclair's tonight, thought you might like to join us."

She glanced back at the computer screen and smiled. "I'd love to, Grandma. Let me change, and I'll be right down."

fifteen

Kavan drove along the charred mountainside, surveying the damage. What was once lush and green from spring rains was now brittle, black, and broken. It would be next spring before life would bloom again.

He could still smell the smoke of the burning forest. Only a few days had gone by since he'd collapsed exhausted on his bed at home, the blaze finally stopped.

He smiled, remembering how he kissed Elizabeth. Her first kiss since Jude McAllister in the fourth grade and on a dollar dare. He chuckled softly. She still exuded some of that grade school innocence, and it charmed his heart.

The town bustled with preparations for the commendation ceremony Friday night. The whole thing made Kavan uneasy. All the attention embarrassed him. After all, he was just doing his job.

In the midst of his contemplation, Travis Knight's deep voice bellowed over the radio sitting on the dash. "Donovan, report in."

Kavan reached for the hand mike. "I'm on my way."

❧

Travis greeted Kavan cordially when he entered his office and sat in the chair across from his desk. But underneath his friendly exterior, Kavan sensed the same anger that had been brewing for weeks.

"How's it feel to be the town hero?" Travis settled in his wide desk chair, a subtle sarcasm laced his words.

Kavan breathed deep. "Uncomfortable, to be honest." From Travis's posture, he could tell the man really had no patience for small talk.

"I'm giving you room on this refurbishment budget deal,

but let me tell you, Kavan. . ." Travis angled forward and pointed his fat finger at the ranger. "I'll turn your hero reputation into that of reprobate overnight if I figure out you've been pilfering the division's money."

Kavan jumped to his feet in one smooth motion. He placed his hands on Travis's desk and lowered his face toward his boss's. "I've told you before, and I'll tell you again, I am not stealing the division's money."

He trembled, using every ounce of self-control to keep himself in check. He wanted to explode at Travis, but he knew it would gain him nothing and only deepen Travis's suspicion of him.

"I don't see any records proving otherwise." Travis cocked his head sideways as if to challenge Kavan.

"My records are in order."

"What happened when your spreadsheet program crashed?"

"I lost my original records."

Travis leaned on the desk and folded his fingers together. "Rather convenient, don't you think?"

Kavan gritted his teeth. "I didn't purposefully crash a computer program, Travis. I had duplicate files at home. They are available for you to see anytime you want to see them."

"Did you doctor those files, Donovan?"

"Don't patronize me, Travis. I'm not a twelve-year-old kid lying his way out of trouble."

Travis stood and walked around the desk. "I've been patient, waiting for you to come clean while I can still help you. Sooner or later, this will be out of my hands. If this turns into an official investigation, you are on your own."

Kavan recognized Travis's intimidation tactics. Yet, he had nothing to confess, nothing to reveal. His records were in order. The whole implication that he would steal and commit forgery angered him. He thought his character and reputation were irrefutable.

He sensed the Spirit of the Lord whisper to him at the moment. *Humble yourself.*

Kavan paused, pondering what to say next.

"Well?" Travis said after a moment.

Taking a deep breath, Kavan said, "I can't confess something I did not do, Travis, but I will submit to whatever process you want me to go through."

Travis's hard exterior softened with surprise. Kavan saw the muscles in his face relax. "Well, uh, why don't you bring in your files from home, and we'll take a look at those. We'll get to the bottom of this, I'm sure."

Kavan turned to leave. "Thank you, Sir."

❧

Elizabeth felt buried under a pile of papers. She'd spent most of the morning daydreaming between Kavan's kiss and heading off to grad school. She'd searched on the Internet for jobs in nuclear energy, and there were plenty available. New government initiatives would expand the field, and by the time she graduated with her master's, lucrative career opportunities would be waiting.

However, she ignored the churning in her stomach every time she thought about school. Dismissing it as nervous energy, she let her thoughts wander back to Kavan.

How sweet he'd been when they finally talked about their kiss. As far as she was concerned, it was about the best first kiss a girl could ever get—sincere, tender, and passionate.

Will peered around the doorway. "You got the quarterly report? We're meeting with the board of directors in a half hour."

Elizabeth snapped back to the present. "Yes. Yes, I do. I just need to call your secretary and ask her a quick question."

Will nodded. "Bring it to the board room when you're done."

Elizabeth dialed Rose's number. "Hi, Rose, it's Elizabeth. I have a question about the quarterly report."

Rose answered without hesitation, and within ten minutes, Elizabeth pulled the report together and rushed it down to Will.

"Thanks, Beth," he said.

Back in her office, Elizabeth took a deep breath and said a short prayer. "Lord, I need to focus. Stop daydreaming about Kavan and get on to my next goal—school."

The phone rang on the trail of her words. "Lambert's Furniture."

"Hi, it's Kavan."

"Hi." Elizabeth's resolve crumbled.

"How are you?"

"Fine. And you?"

"Tired of all this hero stuff."

Elizabeth laughed. "Typical White Birch, don't you think?"

"Yes. Guess that's why I love this town." He chuckled. "I just wish it wasn't focused on me."

"Well, if you ask me, you deserve it."

"The only way I can endure it is if you will accompany me to Friday night's ceremonies."

She answered without hesitation. "I'd love to, Kavan."

"Elizabeth," he started. She heard the seriousness in his tone. "This is a date."

She chewed her bottom lip and played with the pencils lined up on her desk. The whole town would see her with him. They'd assume. . .

"Well," she paused, "as long as you don't kiss me in front of everyone. . ."

Kavan's laughter floated over the line. "I promise."

"Okay, then." She felt like a schoolgirl.

"I'll pick you up at seven."

"Six-thirty," she countered.

He chuckled. "Six-thirty. I gotta go. Need to get some stuff for Travis. The refurbishment debacle won't go away."

"Really? I'm sure you'll figure it out."

"I'm praying so. I can only lean on the Lord on this one. It's a puzzler."

"See ya."

"Friday."

After she hung up, Elizabeth stared blankly at the wall.

What was I thinking, saying yes to him? The whole town will whisper about us. The family will tease me with "love and marriage" remarks.

Hmm. . . For the first time, she realized she didn't care. The idea didn't petrify her, and she rather enjoyed the junior high jitters dancing in her middle.

Enough, Elizabeth. Back to work. Diving into accounts payable, Elizabeth worked steadily for several hours.

A collection of invoices surfaced from the Division of Forests and Lands. All of them like the ones she'd seen before. Cuts of expensive wood, all bearing Kavan's name.

She shook her head, withstanding the urge to assume. *What are you doing, Kavan?*

Elizabeth printed the invoices and placed them one by one on a worktable. She studied them, hands on her hips. After a moment, she moved to the filing cabinet and pulled the division's purchase orders. One by one, she matched purchase order and invoice. Hunching over, she examined each set.

Kavan's signature caught her attention. She smiled, liking the funny way he made his *K*s. That purchase order and invoice, dated in March, was for a load of pine. *Typical orders, according to Mr. Hansen.*

Her gaze moved to the next set of papers. "Oh, no," she whispered, picking up the purchase order for a closer examination. The order called for a load of teak, and while the bottom line carried Kavan's name, it was not his signature.

Swiftly, she found all the purchase orders that did not have Kavan's signature. She arranged them by date and moved to the copier.

Several minutes later, she dialed Kavan's cell phone. *No answer.* She read the Division of Forests and Lands' phone number from their account in the computer and dialed the office. "He's not here," a woman said, overly sweet.

Fumbling through the phone book, Elizabeth looked up his home phone number. *Kavan, be home, please.*

The busy signal beeped in her ear. *Busy.*

Elizabeth grabbed her purse, the copied stack of purchase orders and invoices, and dashed out the door.

ta-

A low growl emanated from Fred. Kavan glanced up from the computer where he was copying his refurbishment report to a floppy. Ginger whined and scratched at the back door.

Kavan listened. "Lay down, Fred. Lay down, Ginger. No one is here." He clicked the printer icon above the spreadsheet. He thought it would be wise to have a hard copy of his spending. . .just in case.

A small knock on the back door sent the dogs into a barking frenzy. Startled, Kavan jumped from his chair.

"Pipe down, you two," he hollered, grabbing the doorknob.

"Elizabeth! Come in." He stepped aside to let her pass.

She came through the door grinning like the Cheshire cat. She plopped her big leather purse on the counter and beamed at Kavan, her sapphire eyes sparkling.

He joined her at the counter, resisting the subtle but sure urge to wrap her up in his arms and greet her with a kiss. He'd kissed her once, but kissing still felt like uncharted territory, and he wanted to proceed cautiously.

"Well, are you going to tell me why you're looking at me like I just won a million dollars, or do I have to guess?"

"I've discovered something," she blurted out.

"Fascinating. A new law of physics?" Kavan leaned as close to her as he could. She smelled like fresh flowers.

"Ha! No."

"Then what?" Kavan folded his arms and regarded her. He loved seeing a new side of Elizabeth.

She pulled a stack of papers out of her purse. Clearing the napkin holder and the salt and pepper shakers from the table, she systematically placed copies of Lambert's Furniture invoices and forestry division purchase orders in front of them.

"Purchase orders?" Kavan asked. "Invoices?"

"POs with your name on them."

Kavan examined the papers. "Two hundred board feet of

cherry." He glanced at Elizabeth. "I never ordered cherry."

"Teak and cedar, too," she said, selecting another purchase order for him to review.

Kavan shook his head. "But that's not my signature."

"Exactly," Elizabeth said. "Kavan Donovan, I am afraid you're being framed."

His gaze met hers. "Come on, Elizabeth, who would do such a thing?"

"I don't know, but someone is charging expensive materials to the forestry division and signing your name. This must be the key to your budget problem." She paused, then added, "Your boss thinks you're embezzling, doesn't he?"

"It sure seems that way. How did you figure this out?" Kavan asked, picking up one of the forged orders. "Some of these date before I even started the refurbishment project."

"I noticed the cherry order one day. I called Grant Hansen to see why we cut several hundred board fet of cherry for the forestry division. He said we still provide millwork to some customers. Your name stood out to me because we'd just met a few days before at Sinclair's."

"Good eye, Lambert. Think I'll call you Eliz-a-sleuth from now on."

She narrowed her eyes at him. "Har, har. Don't even think about it. I'll take my evidence and leave you to your own measly devices."

Kavan cleared his throat, pretending to be threatened by her words. "How did you know it wasn't my signature?"

"Remember how I thought your *K*s were unusual? I noticed it when you signed the debit card receipt the first time we went to Giuseppe's."

Kavan looked at her and let his gaze linger on her face for a moment. "I can't thank you enough."

She reached out and tenderly touched his arm. "Anything for a friend."

Kavan pulled her to him and brushed her cheek lightly with the back of his fingers. Without a word, he kissed her.

After the kiss, she looked up at him, a spark in her blue eyes. "Are you always going to kiss me without warning?"

"Maybe." He winked.

"I'll be on guard, then." She gathered up the purchase orders and returned them to the folder. "Come on, let's go show your boss. I can't wait to see the look on his face."

sixteen

Kavan walked into the Division of Forests and Lands office like he owned the world, Elizabeth by his side.

"Cheryl, is Travis in?"

She nodded but narrowed her dark eyes at him. "Who's your friend?"

"Elizabeth, this is Cheryl."

The women greeted each other. Kavan stepped over to Travis's office and rapped his knuckles lightly on the heavy wooden door.

"Come in."

Kavan stepped through, motioning for Elizabeth to follow. The heavyset director studied him, waiting. He considered them with his hands clasped together on his round belly as if he expected a show.

Kavan dropped the signed purchase orders and invoices on Travis's desk.

"What's this?" Travis asked, reaching for one of the papers.

"That's not my signature, Travis."

Travis glanced at Kavan, indifference in his eyes.

"Someone is ordering teak, walnut, mahogany, and cherry from Lambert's Furniture and charging it to the fire tower account. They signed the POs with my name."

Travis moved to review the documentation, his brow raised. Kavan knew he finally had his attention.

"How did you come across this?" Travis examined each of the forms.

Kavan introduced Elizabeth and explained her discovery. "She recognized my signature. Look, on those purchase orders." Kavan pointed to the ones with his legitimate signature. "The lumber is pine. That's all I've used on the fire tower."

"You're telling me somebody ordered lumber and charged it to your refurbishment account," Travis summarized.

"Yes," Kavan said without hesitation. "There are also some that were charged to the general department expenses before the fire tower project was even approved."

Travis picked through the orders again. Suddenly a shadow fell over his face. Quickly, he flipped through several of the pieces, then stacked them neatly together. He stood. "May I keep these, Miss Lambert?"

"Those are copies." Elizabeth glanced sideways at Kavan. "You can keep them." Kavan watched her trying to suppress her beautiful smile.

A heavy silence hung in the air. Travis remained focused on the forged purchase orders, his hands idly stacking them over and over. "Well, Donovan, looks like you've managed to clear your name."

Kavan nodded. "Yes, Sir." He extended his hand to Travis.

It took a second, but the older man grasped his hand in a firm shake. "I'll take it from here. You keep working on that old White Birch fire tower."

"If you don't mind, I think I'll wait until the dust settles." Kavan eyed his boss. Travis had obviously seen something in those papers that bothered him. But Kavan knew better than to ask.

Outside, he laughed and grabbed Elizabeth in a swirling hug. "Thank you! I feel like I've lost a thousand pounds."

Once he landed her feet back on the ground, he kissed her again with enthusiasm.

Elizabeth stepped out of his embrace. "I can't believe you," she said, her tone sharp, her blue eyes sparking.

Kavan stared at her for a moment. "What? I told you I'd kiss you without warning."

"I can't believe you let Travis Knight off so easy. He all but accused you of stealing. Stealing, Kavan." She glared at him with her hands on her hips. "He questioned your integrity. And you let him off with a howdy-do handshake. He didn't even apologize!"

Her ire stirred his. "What'd you want me to do, slap him around?"

"Demand an apology. A written apology."

"What? Elizabeth, he was mistaken. Quite frankly, I can understand—"

"Your career and reputation are on the line, Kavan. Stick up for yourself." Elizabeth turned and marched toward the truck.

Kavan raced after her and grabbed her arm. He pulled her aside and peered into her face. "My reputation and career is not mine to defend. The Lord will look out for me. He's done so much already. How Christlike would it be if I sought revenge or retribution?"

"I could never let it go that easy."

"The Lord gives grace to the humble, Elizabeth."

To his surprise, tears glistened in her eyes. "Let's go," she whispered.

They drove in silence to his house. Slanted rays of late afternoon sunlight glanced over White Birch, and the serenading song of the crickets filled their ears. When Kavan pulled into the gravel drive, Fred and Ginger hailed them with a barking chorus.

"What's bothering you, Elizabeth?" Kavan stopped the truck, shifted into park, and shut off the engine.

She faced him and said with passion, "That you are just letting this go. You're letting it happen, not sticking up for yourself."

He glared at her. "Well, I don't see it that way. The Lord resolved the issue—"

"With my help. If I hadn't found those purchase orders and receipts, you'd still be suspect."

"Hold on there, Elizabeth. Yes, you were the key to this whole mystery, but the Lord unlocked the door in the first place. He could have done it without you."

Elizabeth got out of the truck and slammed the door.

Kavan bounded out of the truck after her. "Where are you going?"

"To take command of my life." She jerked open the door to the VW and climbed in.

"Elizabeth, what's going on?" He looked through the open passenger side window. "Obviously this is about more than Travis Knight and the case of forged signatures."

She cocked her head to look at him. "You're right. It's about me, Elizabeth Lambert, taking charge of my life."

Kavan watched her drive away. He resisted the urge to chase after her, certain she would not welcome his prodding. "Lord, You speak to her. Comfort her."

❧

"Grandma, I'll be in my room," Elizabeth said as she entered the kitchen.

Grandma glanced up from the kitchen table where she read her Bible. "You're home early. Everything okay?"

"Any mail for me today?"

"Nooo," Grandma answered, drawing out the word.

Muttering to herself, Elizabeth entered her room. She pulled up the window shades to let in the day's remaining light and booted up her laptop.

"Let my relationship with Kavan distract me. . . And Grandpa's story about Harvard and a pregnant wife. . . Thinking I could live in this town. . . Who cares about school? Me. I'm going to find out what's going on with my applications."

Checking her E-mail, she found nothing new regarding her graduate school status.

Determined to find answers, she hopped onto the Internet and found Ohio State's admissions page. She clicked on the link for graduate students. Finding a telephone number, she reached for the phone.

A nervous trill came out of her throat as the phone rang and someone answered.

"Hi, my name is Elizabeth Lambert. I'd like to check on my graduate school application." She listened for a moment, then spelled her name and gave her social security number. "Yes, I'll hold."

You bet I'll hold. I'm going to find out what's going on.

She tapped her fingernails on the base of her laptop, staring out the window. Grandpa strolled up the drive with Ethan's golden retriever, Hutch. Elizabeth smiled.

"Miss Lambert?"

"Yes?" Elizabeth returned her focused to the call.

"Your application was denied."

Elizabeth resisted the urge to scream and asked through clenched teeth, "Yes, I know. But why?"

"I don't know." Irritation laced the woman's voice. "I—oh, wait. You didn't submit your transcripts from MIT."

Elizabeth stood so fast her desk chair tipped over. "What?"

"You didn't send us your undergraduate transcripts."

"I paid for the university to send them."

"Well, we didn't get them."

Elizabeth circled the room in small steps. "What do you mean you didn't get them?"

The woman answered slowly, tossing out her words one at a time, "We...did...not...get...them. They never arrived."

With a sigh, Elizabeth thanked the woman and hung up. After another quick search on the Internet, she found South Carolina's and Michigan's information. Quick calls to their admissions departments yielded the same result. MIT had not submitted her transcripts.

Stunned, Elizabeth sat on the edge of her bed, blinking back tears while her middle bubbled with a giggle. Denied admittance due to a clerical error.

How classic.

She took a second to mull the situation over, then got on the computer. A plan formed in her head while she fired off a few E-mails and checked all the universities' Web sites for application deadlines. Perhaps she still had time. . . .

The sunlight faded, and shadows appeared in the corners of her room. Grandpa appeared in the doorway. "Dinner's on, Kitten."

Elizabeth glanced around at him with a smile. "MIT didn't send my transcripts."

"What?"

"MIT didn't send my transcripts. That's why my grad school applications have been denied."

Grandpa laughed. "Don't that beat all? How'd you find out?"

"I took command," she said. Linking her arm with his, Elizabeth walked with Grandpa to the kitchen, and during dinner, she regaled her grandparents with the events of the day.

❧

Kavan rang the doorbell. Nervous, he mentally rehearsed what he wanted to say. He couldn't rest until he'd squared things with Elizabeth. He'd prayed and prayed about it, but still couldn't find resolve within himself. Funny, he didn't have the urge to make a defense before Travis and the New Hampshire Division of Forests and Lands, but, did want to explain his actions to Elizabeth. He couldn't bear the idea of her perceiving him as a coward or a weakling.

The door to the Lamberts' kitchen flew open, and a smiling, bubbly, all too beautiful Elizabeth stood there.

"Kavan," she gushed, throwing her arms around him. "You're just in time for dessert. Are you hungry?"

Shocked, yet amused, Kavan stepped inside. "I'd never turn down a Grandma Betty dessert."

Elizabeth led him to the table, his hand in hers. Grandpa Matt congratulated him on his forgery find while Grandma Betty slid a large slice of iced applesauce cake under his nose. Elizabeth chatted merrily about the strange signatures on the purchase orders and how they presented the material to Travis Knight.

"Our girl is full of discoveries today." Grandma handed Kavan a cup of coffee.

"Thank you." He took the cup, then fixed his gaze on Elizabeth. "What other discoveries have you made?"

Elizabeth related the story of the missing transcripts, the details punctuated with little points made by her grandparents.

Finally, Elizabeth concluded, "Tomorrow, I'm calling MIT to straighten this thing out."

Kavan looked at her and thought she was actually beaming. He was proud of her, yet disappointed.

So, this is what the Bible means when it says love does not seek its own. Kavan intuitively understood he had to let Elizabeth go.

Grandpa Matt and Grandma Betty excused themselves from the table and wandered arm in arm from the kitchen.

"Well, you're off." Kavan reached for Elizabeth's hand. He loved its velvety texture.

She placed her other hand on top of his. "You always knew that was the plan."

He nodded. "Yes, I did."

"I'm sorry I was so snippy earlier."

Kavan looked up and smiled. He caught her blue gaze with his own. "Don't worry about it. I am so grateful to be out of that mess, and I have you to thank."

"Glad to help, Friend."

Kavan leaned forward, and with his fingertips, touched the side of her face. "Sure you want to leave?"

"I never planned to stay."

"And what does your Friend Jesus say?"

Elizabeth pulled her hand free and rested against the back of her chair. She focused on Kavan for a second before answering. "I don't know, but when I took command of my own situation, I found the answers. Maybe He helped me today like He did you."

"That's one way to look at it." At that moment, Kavan ached. Ached for Elizabeth, for a life with her. "I'm going to miss you."

"I'm going to miss you. But hey, I'm not gone yet. I'll be here another four to six weeks."

"And Friday night, you're my date to the big to-do about nothing ceremony."

"I can't wait." She smiled and kissed him lightly on the cheek.

seventeen

The White Birch Community Center hummed with excited voices. Elizabeth sat among the families and guests of the honored firefighters, watching as Kavan Donovan received a commendation for leadership and bravery.

Her cheeks twinged from the constant smiling. When Kavan walked across the stage, the crowd in the auditorium cheered. His gaze fell on her, and he smiled with a wink. Elizabeth winked back and gave him two thumbs-up.

When he stopped at the podium to speak, Elizabeth imagined her heart might thump right out of her chest.

"Jesus said," Kavan began when the din died down, "that no greater love is there than this, that one would lay down his life for his friends."

The tranquil sound of his voice, combined with his opening statement, captivated Elizabeth.

"Up on that ridge, I did what any of these men would have done. I'm proud to be numbered among them. Mostly, I hope that in some small way I represented Jesus up there and honored His name with my actions. He is our greatest Friend." He paused and looked out over the crowd. "Thank you for honoring us today."

He returned to his seat, accompanied by a symphony of applause.

After the ceremony, Kavan wove through the crowd to Elizabeth. She hugged him with vigor. "I'm so proud! You are a gifted speaker."

"Thanks." He gently cupped her elbow with his hand and steered her through the throng. "I said five sentences. Can't mess that up, Elizabeth."

She laughed. "True, but you looked so calm and stately."

Kavan looked down at her, flashing his hooked grin. "Stately? Now that's a new one." He stopped to hug some ladies and shake hands with several men. As many as could reach him patted him on the back and belted out their congratulations.

Finally, they were outside, breathing in the warm July night air. Stars twinkled down at them.

"I'm hungry," Kavan said. "Let's eat."

"Giuseppe's?" Elizabeth asked, her hand in his as they trotted to his truck.

"Sounds great."

They laughed and talked the whole way to the pizza place, rehashing the tributary events. Kavan declared he never wanted to go through that again.

"The fire or the tribute?" Elizabeth asked, a lilt in her voice.

"Both," Kavan said.

She watched him watching her out the corner of his eye. *If I were ever going to get married, Kavan, it would be to a man like you.*

"You're quiet all of a sudden," Kavan said with a glance her way. He turned into Giuseppe's parking lot.

"Just thinking." Feeling caught by her own thoughts and sublime desire, she looked out the window and up at the mountain.

"About what?" Kavan cut off the engine and shifted his torso toward her.

About what? I can't tell him what I've been thinking. So, she fudged a little. "About the future, school and all. MIT should have sent out my transcripts by now."

"Oh," he said, sounding sad. "I was wondering. . . ." He stopped and looked out the windshield.

Elizabeth's pulse quickened. "You were wondering?"

"Nothing. Let's eat," he said.

Nothing? What were you going to say? She waited for him to open her door. Sliding out of the truck, she slipped into his embrace. His kiss was warm, determined, and made Elizabeth's knees weak. The feel of his lips touching hers lingered for the rest of the night.

Elizabeth hummed softly to herself as she readied for her Saturday afternoon shift at Sinclair's. Showered and dressed in her Sinclair's uniform, she curled up on her bed with one of Grandma's ham sandwiches on homemade bread.

Since last night, she could not forget the feel of Kavan's arms around her and the touch of his kiss.

She took a small bite of her sandwich, then set her plate on the corner of her desk. A picture of Kavan flashed across her mind, causing a giggle to erupt from deep inside. She covered her mouth with a swift move of her hand, shifting her eyes to peek around the room as if someone could have overheard.

So, this is the feeling that moved the pens of the great poets. The emotion that stirred singers to sing and dancers to dance, she thought. Her heart felt light and airy. Peaceful. The feeling began to seem familiar, to become a part of her. And she liked it.

Suddenly, Elizabeth jumped to her feet and stood in the middle of her bed. Thrusting her arms wide, she belted out the first song that came to mind. "The hills are alive with the sound of music."

She crumpled to the bed, laughing.

Grandpa and Grandma appeared in the doorway. "And she tries to tell you *I'm* crazy," Grandpa said to Grandma.

"I'm sorry, you guys; I'm just feeling a little wacky today."

"Wacky? Is that what you kids call it these days? In my day, we called it being in love." Grandpa gazed at his granddaughter over the rim of his wire spectacles.

"In love? As in *falling* in love? Grandpa, you're certifiable. Grandma, watch him." Elizabeth reached over the edge of the bed for her shoes, unable to control the big grin sweeping across her face. "I'm excited that my life is finally moving forward. Grad school is on the horizon, the light at the end of the tunnel."

"Right," Grandpa said, propped against the door, his arms folded over his chest. "Studying physics and math, cramming for tests, working late nights, and getting up early always made me sing at the top of my lungs, too."

Elizabeth hopped up and yanked her purse from the hook on the wall. "No time for your delirium, Grandpa. Sinclair's awaits." She kissed her grandma on the cheek and hugged her grandpa on her way through the door.

"Beth, your sandwich. . . ," Grandma called after her.

"Save it for later. I'm not hungry," she called, waving from the bottom of the stairs with a flutter of her hand.

෨

Kavan strolled down Main Street toward the diner, his mind set on a late supper. He'd felt restless sitting at home, an unusual sensation for him. His cabinlike abode was his sanctuary, and he loved being there. But tonight. . .

He drove past Sinclair's, expecting to see Elizabeth's candy apple red Bug in the parking lot. He did but decided not to stop. As much as he wanted to see her, he needed time to think.

Last night's commendation ceremony—combined with an enchanting evening with Elizabeth—marked one of the best nights of his life. Despite his embarrassment over the hero hoopla, he couldn't help feeling honored by the town's expression of appreciation. Even his parents wired congratulations from Florida.

He smiled, recalling his father's words. *Congratulations, Son. We are proud of you. Warm wishes, Dad and Mom.*

They maintained their physical distance, but Kavan knew they loved him, and their hearts were close. He'd settled that in his mind a long time ago.

"Where to, Lord?" he asked absently after he parked the truck and started down Main Street.

Diner.

"Okay," Kavan said. "Dinner with You tonight, Jesus."

As he walked past the bookstore, mulling over the diner menu, a sparkle in the window of Earth-n-Treasures, Designs by Cindy Mae caught his attention.

Stop.

Kavan halted, then took a step toward the storefront. He studied the items in the display window, various pieces designed from gold and silver. All exquisite. He admired one gold filigree ring hosting a uniquely cut solitaire diamond.

"Hi, Kavan."

He looked up to see the owner of Earth-n-Treasures standing beside him.

"Hi, Cindy Mae. What are you doing in town on a Saturday evening?"

She grinned and shifted the weight of her large frame. "Brill took the kids to a movie, so I thought I'd come in and do a little work."

Kavan glanced up and down Main Street. "I forgot how dead this place is on the weekends."

"We roll up the sidewalks Friday at 5 P.M. until Monday at 8 A.M.," Cindy Mae said, twirling the ends of her thick blond braid between her fingers.

Kavan laughed outright. Cindy Mae painted a true picture of White Birch. "I came in for some dinner," he told her.

Cindy Mae nodded toward the diner. "Sam's the only one who does much business on the weekends."

Kavan agreed. "Can't beat his meat loaf." Next, he motioned to the piece behind the glass. "That's an unusual ring."

"Isn't it beautiful? It's one of the few pieces I didn't make myself." Cindy Mae invited him into the shop to take a closer look. "It's a century old, and that's the original one-karat diamond."

Kavan raised a brow and whistled.

Cindy Mae pointed to the intricate design of the ring's mount with the long tip of her pinky fingernail. "The ring is in classic Edwardian design. Thus, the filigree."

"It's amazing. I've never seen a diamond like this one."

"It's an Asscher cut. Very sought-after cut of diamond in its day," Cindy said, peering up at Kavan. "Still is."

In that instant, somehow Kavan knew he had to purchase the ring. It seemed to symbolize Elizabeth to him, a rare and beautiful find. She was valued by the Lord and valued by him.

"The ring comes with a story, too." Cindy Mae pulled up a

stool and motioned for Kavan to sit.

He listened as Cindy Mae told her tale. "My great-uncle John Ashton bought this ring for the woman he loved in 1904. She accepted the ring, but never wore it, telling Uncle John she wanted to consider his proposal for awhile. A year passed without an answer, so Uncle John pressed his hopeful bride-to-be to set a date. She confessed that she loved another and returned the ring."

For a split second, Kavan imagined he felt the disappointment of John Ashton. "He must have been devastated."

Cindy Mae rested against a glass case and crossed her arms over her middle. "Heartbroken. Family lore has it that he buried himself in work. Made a million dollars, which for his day was a considerable amount. He never married and left the ring in a safety-deposit box he never bothered to tell anyone about."

"Guess he truly wanted to forget," Kavan offered.

Cindy Mae chuckled deeply. "I'm sure he did. He died in the late sixties. My father received the ring as part of his estate, but he was already engaged to my mother, who viewed the ring as bad luck and refused to ever wear it. Recently, Dad brought the ring to me and said to do what I wanted with it. After forty years, he's caved in to my mother's superstitions."

Kavan's heartbeat quickened. Surely someone else in Cindy Mae's family would want the ring. He said as much to his hostess.

She shook her head, disagreeing. "There's only my sister and me now. For some odd reason, we believe this ring belongs to someone besides us. Someone very special, we just don't know who."

Kavan blurted out, "Cindy Mae, how much?" His gaze darted between her face and the ring.

What am I doing?

She did not appear fazed by his question. "You have someone special in your life?"

Kavan chuckled and ran his hand over the top of his hair. "I'm working on it. She just doesn't know it yet."

"Is it the Lamberts' granddaughter?"

"You've seen her," Kavan said.

"She's a fine girl. Beautiful."

Shivers ran down Kavan's back, and his palms grew moist. With a jerky, forward motion, he placed the ring on the front counter. "How much, Cindy Mae?" He braced to hear thousands of dollars. He couldn't imagine how much an antique ring of this caliber would cost. The stone alone had to be worth. . . What? His head started spinning.

Cindy Mae picked up the rare jewel and walked behind the counter. Kavan hoped she wouldn't ring it up without telling him the price. As best he figured, he could spend about five thousand dollars. Even that would just about wipe out his savings.

He waited for Cindy Mae's answer while she worked on the ring, cleaning and polishing it. Then she placed it in a deep blue velvet box, the same color as Elizabeth's eyes.

"Here." She extended her hand, the box on the tip of her fingers. "I knew I didn't come into town tonight to balance the books."

Kavan gaped at her. He tried to answer, but no words would come. "Cindy Mae, I don't understand," he managed to say after a moment.

"Kavan, I don't know why, but I believe with all my heart, you and your girl are the couple for this ring."

"You must be joking. That ring must be worth—"

"Nothing without the right owner." She winked. "Otherwise, it's coal and metal."

"Cindy Mae, I—I don't know. . . I can't—"

"What's your girl's name? I'm drawing a blank."

"She's not my girl. We're good friends, but I don't think you could say she's my girl."

"What's her name?" Cindy Mae repeated.

Kavan stopped and stared at her. Gently he said, "Elizabeth. Elizabeth Lambert."

Cindy clapped her hands, tossed back her head, and

laughed from the core of her belly. "Of course! Now I know this ring belongs to you! The woman my uncle bought the ring for was one Miss Elizabeth Clarke. This ring was purchased for an Elizabeth. Only a century too soon."

Kavan gripped the box. It felt hot in his hand. "Cindy Mae, I don't even know if I'm going to marry her. I mean, I've asked the Lord about it—"

"Well, there you go. The Lord your God knows." Cindy motioned toward the ceiling with her index finger.

"I can't take this," Kavan said with force and conviction. "Not if I don't know if I'll ever marry her!"

Cindy Mae walked around the shop, shutting off lights and covering her art with dustcovers. "Kavan, it's yours. You and God work out the rest."

In a few minutes, they were out of the shop, and Cindy Mae hugged him good-bye.

Dazed, Kavan walked into the diner, his appetite completely diminished. He picked a quiet corner and slid into the booth.

In his breast pocket, the weight of the little blue box burned against his heart.

❧

Friday night, Elizabeth sat in the cozy living room, surrounded by Lamberts trying to decide which movie to watch.

"I brought a romantic comedy." Julie held up her DVD.

"Oh no," Will lamented. "Ethan, do something about your wife."

Ethan laughed and held up his movie. "I brought suspense."

A chorus of female voices erupted. "We watched suspense last time," Ella reminded the men.

Elizabeth turned around to see her cousin Bobby's wife. She'd always loved Ella, so elegant and sophisticated.

Twins Bobby and Will debated over watching an action movie or classic drama. Elizabeth smiled to herself. *How could two people who looked exactly alike be so different?*

For the first time since she came to White Birch and her

grandparents' house, she felt at home and at peace. She didn't mind being an intricate part of the Lambert clan, answering their questions about her life and grad school. In fact, it made her feel treasured and special.

"I'm so excited for you." Julie flopped down on the couch next to her, cozying up to her like intimate sisters.

"Amazing, isn't it." Elizabeth leaned in close to Julie. "I never paid for the transcripts to be sent."

Ethan stooped down and said, "It's almost as if you didn't want them to be sent."

"Ethan!" Elizabeth said, incredulous.

"Hush, you." Julie said, giving his arm a loving tap.

"Get your snacks and drinks. I'm pushing PLAY in two minutes," Grandpa announced.

Everyone made a mad scramble to the kitchen and the bathroom.

Elizabeth remained put, Ethan's comment replaying through her head. *Did I subconsciously not want the transcripts to be sent?* She shifted her position on the couch and chewed her bottom lip.

"Ready, ladies and gentlemen?" Grandpa asked in his lighthearted master of ceremonies tone.

"Hit PLAY," Elizabeth said, grinning at him.

"Where's Kavan?" Grandpa asked.

"Home, I guess."

"Don't you want to invite him? I'll wait."

Elizabeth shook her head. She hadn't seen Kavan much this week, between his schedule and hers. She pictured his handsome face, alive with expressive eyes and his white, hooked smile.

Suddenly she missed him.

Grandpa started the movie. Elizabeth gave her seat to Ethan. "Sit by your wife."

"Where you going?" Julie asked, cuddling up next to Ethan.

"I'll sit by Grandma," Elizabeth answered.

Instead, she stood by the door and waited until the family

became engrossed in the movie, a classic drama. She slipped out the front door and followed the silvery light of the moon to the covered bridge.

Once the transcript situation was straightened out, she'd finally felt relieved. She'd taken command and put her life into gear again.

Now she wondered. A subtle but sure uneasiness floated through her consciousness when she thought about leaving White Birch—when she thought about leaving Kavan.

The bubbling, excited feelings she felt a week ago for Kavan had settled into something solid at the core of her heart.

"Lord," she prayed, "grad school? How can I *not* go? I have to go."

For the first time since her talk with Grandpa, the verse he quoted out of 1 Peter came to mind. " 'Young men, in the same way be submissive to those who are older. All of you, clothe yourselves with humility toward one another, because, "God opposes the proud but gives grace to the humble." ' "

"Lord, give me grace." Elizabeth continued to pour out her heart, believing her Lord and Friend would direct her path.

eighteen

The ring sat on the kitchen counter. It seemed to Kavan that every fiber of his being was drawn to that velvet box every time he passed by, even in the dark of night.

Cindy Mae's gift still amazed him. "Lord, how did You move her to give so extravagantly?" he asked one night, sitting on the back porch, a cold soda bottle in his hand.

He sensed the Lord respond, *Because of My extravagant love for you.*

Kavan smiled at the remarkable working of his Lord, so kind and generous. Yet, he still did not know his next move. In his estimation, he had a ring, but no girl. Elizabeth never even remotely hinted that she would consent to marry him if he asked.

Kavan took a swig of his soda. How to win Elizabeth's heart remained a mystery to him.

He'd stopped by Sinclair's on his way home one evening after spotting her car in the parking lot. Her blue eyes twinkled with merriment when she saw him strolling across the front of the store.

"Hi ya, Gorgeous." He leaned on the front counter.

"Hi ya." She grabbed his hands. "Guess what?"

Her enthusiasm engaged his heart. "Joann gave you a raise," he teased.

Joann stood within earshot. "Ha! Don't we all wish."

Elizabeth glanced at Joann. "Thank you, how kind." Then she aimed her sparkling smile at him. "MIT sent me an E-mail confirming that my transcripts have been sent."

Kavan stiffened, squeezing her hand a little. "Oh, really?"

"Did I tell you?"

"Tell me what?"

"That the reason they were never sent is because I never paid for them to be sent."

"Doesn't sound like you." Kavan's mouth felt as dry as a cotton ball.

"I guess with the pressure of finals and filing applications, I forgot."

"Are you sure it's not too late for admittance?" Kavan thought his tone sounded a little too hopeful.

She shook her head. "No, I checked, and I'm squeaking in under the deadline."

"Well, you'll be on your way soon." Kavan fought the desire to beg her to stay.

Elizabeth's eyes peered steadily into his. "Yep, on my way."

&

Sitting on his porch now, recalling that night, Kavan wondered about the tone in her voice. Did he hear an echo of doubt?

He stood and paced the length of the porch. Maybe he just imagined her doubt because that is what he wanted. And the whole ring thing. . . He sighed and propped himself against the porch rail. Fred whined and curled up by Kavan's feet.

None of it made sense to him. *Lord, why would You give me this ring? You've worked it out for Elizabeth to go to graduate school.*

The idea hit him that maybe the ring was for Elizabeth, just not now. Perhaps after she graduated.

He moaned. That would mean two more years. He'd only known her two months, but it felt like a lifetime. She fit with him. They belonged together.

Tell her.

The simple instruction sliced through his anxious thoughts.

Tell her what? Marry me? Don't follow your dreams? I can't do that. I love her too much.

Kavan didn't want to argue with the Lord, but he lacked courage. Fighting a fire up on the ridge paled in comparison to telling a beautiful, curly-haired brunette he wanted to spend the rest of his life with her. That idea terrified him.

What if she said no? How would he recover and keep their friendship?

"O Lord," he said with a quivering laugh, "I used to consider myself a man of faith, but this is a whole new terrain for me."

No tangible answer came from heaven except a sense of peace and the pleasure of God.

The sound of the phone's ring jolted him out of his deep thought and prayer.

Kavan dashed through the screen door, the sound of its slam following him into the kitchen.

The blue velvet box caught his attention once again.

"Kavan, Travis Knight here."

"Evening, Travis."

"I just came from a meeting down in Manchester. Your name's cleared. The division is investigating the embezzlement."

"Any clues so far?"

"Yes, but they aren't saying much. Possibility that it involves some higher-ups. Apparently, these things are dealt with quietly, and the person is dismissed without prosecution."

Kavan blew a shrill whistle. "Well, I'm glad I'm in the clear. I don't want to know what happens to the other guy."

"Well, you probably will eventually anyway. But, yep, you are in the clear, Son. I'm sorry I doubted you."

"No problem, Travis."

"Have a good weekend."

"You, too." Kavan pressed the button to disconnect. He moved to place the cordless phone on its base, then paused. He had an idea.

He pressed TALK and dialed. Before the first ring, he hung up. He took a deep breath, pressed REDIAL, and set the phone to his ear. It rang once before he hung up again.

He laughed at himself. "This is worse than high school," he said to Fred, who peered at him through the screen door. The dog answered with one deep bark.

"Go for it? Is that what you're saying, Boy? Be like you? Bold?"

Here goes. He sat on a stool at the kitchen counter, shoving the ring box out of sight.

He pressed REDIAL. She answered on the second ring.

"Elizabeth? Hi, it's Kavan."

❧

The chime of Elizabeth's cell phone reverberated under the bridge's cover. The display flashed Kavan's home number. She finished the last of her prayer and answered.

"Hi," she said, a little too softly, a little too intimately. The sound of her own voice caused her to stand at attention. *What is it about girls that they turn to mush when a boy calls?* She steadied herself and lowered her tone. "How are you?"

"Doing well. Travis just called. I'm all cleared. Appears that some higher-ups in the division might be the source of the embezzlement."

"Really?" Excitement spiked her voice. "But your name is completely cleared."

"According to Travis."

"Well, you know how well you can trust him."

"Elizabeth!" Kavan said, both shock and humor in his tone.

"Sorry, I just don't like when people I love. . ." She stopped, unable to believe the words that just flowed out of her mouth. "Well, when people I care about, you know, my friends and family, are falsely accused."

Kavan remained silent for a moment too long.

Why did I say that?

"That's understandable, Elizabeth. Anyway, that's not the main reason I called."

Her insides fluttered. "What's up?"

"I wondered if you, um, well, would you like to go to dinner?"

She wondered at his nervousness, all the while amused by her own jitters. The hand that held her cell phone to her ear trembled slightly. "You know I love Giuseppe's."

"Right, well, not Giuseppe's."

"Then where?"

"Italian Hills."

"That fancy restaurant up on the hill?" The romantic

atmosphere of Italian Hills was legendary in the New England area.

"Yes, the fancy place on the hill."

The tone of his voice, the decisive way he spoke, told Elizabeth this was no ordinary dinner. She panicked. "Kavan, I'm going to school. In about a month."

"So I've heard. All the more reason to enjoy the days that are left."

"With romantic dinners?"

"Who said anything about romantic dinners?" Kavan's voice rose sharply. He sounded flustered.

Elizabeth walked out from under the bridge, into the light of the moon. "Italian Hills is synonymous with romance."

"I like their fettuccine. If you don't want to go, I'll go by myself."

"Oh now, that's ridiculous. When do you want to go?" She climbed the hill to the house.

"Tomorrow night. Saturday."

"What time?"

"Six."

"Six-thirty."

His mellow chuckle tingled in her ear. "See you then."

"See you then."

❧

Elizabeth was grateful for a day at Sinclair's. It kept her mind off her date with Kavan, or so she thought.

"Elizabeth," Joann called, coming out of the back office. "I recounted the cashiers' money bags and not one of them has the right starting bundle."

"What?" Elizabeth turned with a jerky motion. "How can that be? I counted those bags myself." She started for the back office. Joann followed.

"I think they're off 'cause your head is someplace else."

Elizabeth gaped at her boss while rubbing her hand along the top of her head. "Nope, my head is right here where I always keep it." She reached for one of the cashiers' bags and removed the cash bundle.

Joann gave her a sly smile. "Better check the clouds, Girlfriend. I think your head is floating out there. You want to tell me what's going on?"

Elizabeth sighed and dropped the cash bag on the counter. "I'm going to dinner with Kavan. Italian Hills." She spilled her fears, confessing that she had feelings for him, but the timing couldn't be more wrong. The invitation to dinner at Italian Hills emanated with his desire for a deeper relationship—she just knew it.

Joann listened, her head bobbing in contemplation. When Elizabeth finished, Joann said, "When are you going to let go and let love?"

"Later. After grad school, you know that."

"But love is at your door now."

Elizabeth narrowed her eyes. "Joann, I'm not throwing away my future because a cute guy looks my way."

With chagrin, Joann retorted, "Lovely. You just let that pride of yours keep you from the best thing that ever happened to you." She stepped forward and grabbed Elizabeth gently by the shoulders. "Surrender, Girl, surrender."

Joann's comments smarted. Only last night she'd cried out to the Lord for His grace in her life. But today, the same old feelings of control emerged. She looked at her boss.

"I'll admit," Elizabeth said, raising one hand, "that I've come to enjoy Kavan's attention and the schoolgirl feelings, but I won't let them govern me. I won't surrender."

"Fine, have it your way. But hear me now," Joann paused, wagging her finger under Elizabeth's nose. "Before this time next year, I'll be dancing at your wedding."

&

Waiting for Kavan to pick her up, Elizabeth paced the living room. Grandpa looked up at her from his chair where he sat reading. "Sit down, Beth. You're making me nervous."

Grandma set aside the book she was reading. "You are making more of this than you need to, Beth." She offered a simple, sincere prayer. "Father, give Beth grace and peace. Reveal Your will to her."

"Thank you, Grandma," Elizabeth said, bending to kiss her grandma's cheek. "How do you always know what I need and how to pray?"

❧

Kavan glanced at the clock. *Six-fifteen! Where did the time go?* He reached for his black leather belt hanging on a hook in his closet. He slipped it through the loops of his dark gray slacks, while yanking a white mock turtleneck from a hanger. He pulled it over his head and quickly finished dressing.

Shoes, where are my shoes? He hunted around the closet floor and under the bed. *Where are my dress shoes?*

In stocking feet, he skidded along the polished wood floor of the living room, looking for his shoes under the sofa and chairs.

Aha. He spotted them in the corner by the bookshelf.

Finally ready, he raced out the door.

My keys!

He dashed back inside. Where were his keys? He looked under the papers on the kitchen counter. The blue velvet box still sat where he'd shoved it yesterday. In the bedroom, he checked his dresser and nightstand.

Of all the times to lose my keys. . . I never lose my keys.

He ducked into the laundry room and rummaged through the basket of dirty laundry. He heard a jingling sound coming from the previous day's work pants. He found his keys in the right front pocket.

Laughing at himself, he dashed for his truck. At 6:35 he pulled into the Lamberts' driveway.

Elizabeth opened the door and greeted him with a smile. "Come in; say hi to Grandpa and Grandma."

Kavan entered. He stooped to Elizabeth's ear as he passed her. "You look incredible."

A pink hue painted her cheeks. "Thank you. You're looking mighty dapper yourself."

He greeted the elder Lamberts, trying to appear relaxed, at ease, but he was sure they could hear the pounding of his heart.

❧

The Italian Hills restaurant sat outside White Birch in the foothills of the White Mountains. As Elizabeth entered the elegant establishment, she felt like a queen on Kavan's arm. With confidence, he gave his name to the maître d' and gently guided her through the candlelit tables to a cozy window table in the corner of the restaurant.

"Kavan." Elizabeth allowed him to hold her chair as she sat down. "This is beautiful."

He sat across from her. "I know. I've only been here once, but this is better than I remember."

"Only once?" she teased. "You love their fettuccine?"

"Yes, it's the only thing I've eaten here."

She chortled, keeping her voice low. The sound of violins grew closer as a quartet strolled toward them. "You always make me laugh."

"Is that a bad thing?"

"No, actually. It's good. I used to laugh a lot, but the stress and competition of school kind of choked out my sense of humor."

Kavan nodded. She knew he understood. Perhaps it was her imagination, but he seemed to understand everything. He was always so patient and kind.

The waiter brought their menus. With polish, he recited the evening's specials. When he'd taken their drink order and gone, Elizabeth leaned toward Kavan and whispered, "I prefer the waitress with the bubble gum."

Kavan chuckled. "She did have a certain charm."

They ordered, and not long after, the waiter brought the plate of appetizers.

"Here, try one of these," Kavan said, dropping a stuffed mushroom onto Elizabeth's plate.

She took a bite, her blue gaze steady on Kavan. "Very good. Best stuffed mushroom I've ever had."

As they ate, their conversation fell into an easy, comfortable rhythm.

They found they had many ideals and desires in common. Despite their Fourth of July nuclear-versus natural-energy debate, they found common ground in faith, love of life, and a fascination with science.

"Yeah, but you're a tree hugger," Elizabeth said, rolling her eyes.

"At least I can hug a tree. When was the last time you hugged a nuclear reactor?"

So, the debate ensued again, but this time with gentleness and respect. When the main course arrived, they'd agreed to disagree.

"After my master's, I'll have more fuel for my fire." She swirled her fork through her fettuccine.

Kavan paused his fork in midair, then set it against his plate. "So, have you decided where you want to go?"

"Whoever asks me first, I'm going."

Suddenly, Kavan dropped his fork and stood to his feet. His napkin fluttered to the floor. Gazing down at her, serious and intent, he asked, "Elizabeth Lambert, will you marry me?"

nineteen

He heard the words come out of his mouth, but he couldn't believe his own ears. Jesus said that, "out of the overflow of the heart the mouth speaks," and at that moment, Kavan understood the deep truth of those words.

Elizabeth stared up at him. Shock masked her face. "What?" she whispered.

Kavan hesitated, desperate to repeat his question while longing for eloquence.

The ring. Why didn't I bring the ring? I didn't know. . . .

But the moment felt so right. A thrill shot through him as he dropped to one knee. "Elizabeth Lambert, will you marry me?"

"You can't be serious."

"Dead serious. You just said, whoever asked first. I'm asking."

She lowered her face to his. "We've never even said 'I love you.' "

Kavan rose from bended knee and sat in the seat next to Elizabeth. He took her hand in his. The food on their plates, shoved to one side, remained untouched. "I know we've never said it, but we feel it. At least I do. I love you, Elizabeth. I love you."

He could not read her emotions from the expression on her face. "Are you going to say anything?" he said after a long, hot pause.

"I don't know what to say. Kavan, I'm going to school. Why did you ask me to marry you?"

He dropped his gaze and studied the delicate lines of her petite, slender hands. "A wise man once said, 'He who finds a wife finds what is good and receives favor from the Lord.' You are a good thing, Elizabeth, and I want to share my life with you."

She would not look into his eyes. Quietly she said, "Please, can we go?"

❧

Midmorning Monday, Kavan drove to the fire tower, his refurbishment project under way again. He expected to meet with the carpenter later that day and finalize construction plans. The embezzlement accusations had soured Kavan on this project, but he wanted it completed before the winter snows.

He inspected the tower as he climbed to the top, making notes in his electronic data assistant. Yet, he paused every few steps, his thoughts trapped in the events of Saturday night.

Elizabeth, oh, Elizabeth, will you ever speak to me again?

He'd driven her home that evening in awkward silence. Neither knew what to say. Convinced he should not pressure her, he'd left her alone to process her emotions. However, he could not retract his question. Perhaps he'd let the romantic ambience of Italian Hills sweep him away momentarily. Perhaps his timing was all wrong, but in his heart of hearts, Kavan wanted to marry the blue-eyed electrical engineer.

He didn't regret the fact that his question would linger on the winds of time for all of eternity. His words still echoed in his mind, along with the story of Cindy Mae's uncle. Maybe his Elizabeth would not wear the ring, either. Kavan winced. He did not want to go the way of Uncle John.

With poise and grace, Elizabeth had avoided answering his question. She'd slipped out of his truck with a hushed "good night" and disappeared in the darkness. He waited until the porch light flashed before starting home.

Immediately, he went to prayer. *Lord, what have I done?*

For a split second, he imagined the Lord's kind smile over him. *Well, you told her.*

Kavan smiled as he drove home. *Oh yes, like a bull in a china shop.*

He had no idea what his next move should be. Sunday, he stayed home and fellowshipped with the Lord in the serenity of his own home. He thought it would be wise to give Elizabeth some space. Her relationship with the Lord was finally blossoming, and he didn't want to make her feel uncomfortable as she worshiped with the rest of the Lord's saints.

He enjoyed his Sabbath day, spending the morning in prayer and contemplation, then running Fred and Ginger through the foothills that afternoon.

Yet, truth be told, his mind never totally disengaged from his longing for Elizabeth. He imagined her sitting next to him in the empty rocker on the back porch, praying with him, talking with him, sharing life with him.

He imagined picnics with her in the shade of the oaks and maples.

❧

Monday evening, Kavan's phone rang, shattering the silence of the house.

Kavan muted the television and reached for the phone.

"Hello."

"Kavan, it's Dad."

He sat forward and checked his surprise. "Dad. Hello. How are you?"

"Fine, Son. July in Miami—can you imagine anything more insane?"

Kavan chuckled. "No, actually."

"Your mother loves it. She's as brown as a buckeye."

"I imagine you're staying cool in the condo with a pile of good books."

Ralph Donovan answered, "Naturally."

"So, what's up?" Momentary concern gripped him. Kavan loved hearing his father's voice, but the man did not call often. "Everything okay?"

"Yes. But I was going to ask you the same thing."

Kavan smiled into the phone, tears burning in his eyes. He stalled them by taking a deep breath. He steadied his voice and said, "Things are, um, good."

"You've been on my mind today." The brief expression

communicated a mountain of words to Kavan. It was his father's unemotional way of telling him he missed him and cared for him. It was also an indication from his heavenly Father that He also loved him and watched over him.

"I talked with Alvin the other night," his father started.

Kavan pictured his father's former business partner. "How is he?"

"Fat and rich. He's making more money than ever. I left the business too soon."

"It happens."

"What's with you and the Lambert girl?" The question came in traditional Ralph Donovan style, without preamble.

"How'd you hear about her?"

"Alvin."

Elizabeth is right. This town is obsessed with romance.

"Nothing is up with the Lambert girl."

"Does she have a name?"

"Elizabeth." Knowing what questions would come next, Kavan recited her résumé. "MIT graduate, electrical engineering, 4.0, applying for graduate schools in nuclear engineering."

"Sounds like a stellar woman."

"She is pretty amazing."

"Well, are you marrying her?"

"No, Dad, I don't think so."

They talked for the better part of an hour, the conversation abating remnants of anxiety and concern over his Saturday actions.

"Bold move, Son. Never regret a bold move," Ralph told him.

Later, as Kavan readied for bed, the sound of his dad's voice echoed in his head. How did His heavenly Father communicate His love so profoundly through his pragmatic, nononsense, earthly father? He considered it a mystery, but a beautiful one.

Just as he clicked off the light, the phone rang again.

"Hello?" Kavan said.

"Hi, it's me."

ta

Elizabeth sat on her bed, the light of her desk lamp illuminating the room in soft gold light, and debated with herself.

Should I call him? No, wait for him to call. He started this. Let him finish it. But he deserves an answer. He asked a sincere question.

Elizabeth glanced at the paper lying on the edge of her desk. Her résumé. Well, what could it hurt to pass it around? She'd heard wonderful things about Creager Electronics and their innovations with robotics.

"What you got there?" Grandpa appeared in the doorway.

Elizabeth looked up, setting aside the résumé. "Hi, Grandpa. I thought you and Grandma were playing bridge."

"We were, but Grant Hansen wasn't feeling well, so we cut the evening short."

"They're nice people, aren't they?" Elizabeth shifted position on her bed so Grandpa could sit on the edge.

"Fine folks." He surveyed the room while reaching for the résumé. Tipping his head upward, he read the neat black print through his bifocals. "Looking for work?"

Elizabeth grabbed a pillow and hugged it to her. "I enjoyed robotics at MIT. I spent a few terms in the artificial intelligence lab. Creager is a leading robotics company."

Grandpa stuck out his chin and scratched his head. "What a coincidence," he said, a lilt in his tone. "Sounds like you got a good plan, Kitten."

Elizabeth couldn't hold it in any longer. "Kavan asked me to marry him."

As usual, Grandpa took the news in stride. "What did you say?"

Tears pooled in her eyes and slipped down her cheeks. She brushed them away with a quick swipe of her fingers. "I told him to take me home."

"Falling in love was not the plan for this summer, was it?"

She shook her head and reached for a tissue, trying to halt the tears. With her eyes fixed on the ceiling, she said, "I'm going to school, Grandpa. I am."

"I hate to sound preachy, Beth, but what is God saying to you? You think this transcript error might have been His doing?"

"No, it was clearly my doing. But I don't know what's what anymore except that I'm frustrated."

"Sometimes the Lord frustrates our plans to get our attention." He gently set the résumé back in its place. "I think Kavan is your *pregnant wife*."

Despite the tears, Elizabeth laughed. "You can't smooth this over with a joke, Grandpa."

"I'm confident the Lord's plans for you are good. I'm confident they include Kavan."

"I wish I had your confidence. I'll feel like a failure if I don't go to grad school."

"I know the feeling. That's why I packed my bags and trotted off to Harvard. But it was my pride, Bethy. Your success is not in what you do, but in who you are in Jesus. His death on the cross, His resurrection life, and His righteousness define you."

"I hear you, Grandpa, and I'm trying to understand that truth more and more. But somehow Jesus dying on the cross doesn't seem to answer the question of school."

"If you are going to school to be considered a success, then you have already failed. Kitten, you are successful because you know Jesus. You realize only ten percent of the world's population claims Him as their Lord and Savior. Look at you, you're in the top ten percent of the world."

She laughed and tapped him on the arm. "You are making it too easy for me to decide against school."

Grandpa nodded and patted Elizabeth's leg. "Only because I'm speaking what you already know in your heart."

Elizabeth bobbed her head in agreement, sighing. "Suddenly, school doesn't seem to be the right path, but I don't know what else to do."

"Marry Kavan."

She let go a wry chuckle. "The one thing I said I'd *never* do. . .let my heart rule my head."

"Well, that motto has merit," Grandpa conceded. "But

either way you go, your heart is ruling your head. The prideful desire to go to grad school will win. Or the sincere desire to know true love. But sometimes the heart touched by love is privileged to make the choice."

"How did you get to be so wise?" Elizabeth asked. She scooted to the end of the bed and stood up. "I'm going down to the bridge to pray."

Grandpa stood and drew her into his embrace. "Good idea. Grandma and I will pray for you here."

Elizabeth slipped on her sneakers and grabbed her phone.

The serenity under the bridge always amazed her. It was as if God waited there for her. As soon as she walked under the cover, she sensed His presence.

Her thoughts and prayers wandered between school and Kavan. The issue did not seem to be a matter of choosing love over education; it seemed more about surrendering her will to God's.

Stubborn pride, she thought.

Leaning against the bridge's strong beam, Elizabeth uttered the words that finally unlocked her heart. "Lord, forgive my pride. I surrender my plans, my heart, to You."

Tears flowed, and doubt began to drain from her as if a big plug had been pulled. She didn't have to fight to be in control. Her Lord controlled her life, and He loved her. He was her Friend, and His plans for her were perfect.

Liberty rang through her body. "I'm free to do God's will, not mine," she shouted.

Kavan. She reached for her phone and dialed.

Her heart throbbed at the sound of his hello.

"Hi, it's me."

❧

Kavan sat up in bed and clicked on the lamp. "How are you?"

He heard a rolling giggle. "I'm fine. Fine. Just fine."

He grinned. "Are you sure?"

"Uh-huh."

Kavan glanced at the alarm clock. "Where are you?"

"On the bridge."

"At eleven o'clock? Elizabeth, it's too late to be out alone." He ran his hand over his closely cropped hair and propped his arms on his knees.

"Grandpa knows I'm out here."

"Wait 'til I see him."

Her light chuckle floated from the phone, a melodic sound he loved.

"I never answered your question," she said.

Now his heart pounded like thundering horses, and he dropped the phone's mouthpiece below his chin, not wanting Elizabeth to hear his labored breathing.

"Look, Elizabeth," he said after a moment, his voice steady. "I'm sorry I surprised you with such a life-altering question, but I meant every word I said."

"I had no doubt. That didn't make it any easier."

Kavan stretched out his legs and leaned against a pile of bed pillows. "You can take your time answering."

"You know you have some nerve messing with a girl's heart and mind."

Kavan listened. He could tell Elizabeth needed to talk. Half of him dreaded the answer he felt sure would come at the end of her monologue, but he needed to know.

"I mean, I come up here to spend a quiet summer with Grandpa and Grandma, to work and prepare for grad school. Instead, you have to come waltzing into my life. A redheaded tree hugger!"

He guffawed. "You think I planned it just to annoy you?"

"If I didn't know you better, yes."

Low and steady, he responded, "I didn't intend on falling in love with a nuke advocate who happens to be so beautiful I see her eyes in the night sky instead of the stars."

"Oh, Kavan, you aren't making this any easier."

"I love you, Elizabeth. I love you. I hate saying that over the phone, but I love you."

The long pause on her end didn't reassure him.

Finally, she whispered, "I have an answer."

He sat up again, so fast all the blood drained from his face and he saw spots. "Yes?"

"Can you meet me on the bridge?"

"When?"

"Friday night."

"That long, eh?"

"I'm sorry, I need to think and pray. Just to be sure."

"Ah, just like a scientist. Analyze everything to death."

"You'll appreciate it later in life."

He grinned, feeling as if she were throwing him a bone of hope. "Friday is fine, my friend."

"See you then."

"What time? Six-thirty?"

She responded with a mock laugh. "Ha, ha. I have to work until ten. Eleven o'clock?"

"Sure."

"Good night."

She hung up before he could respond. But in an instant, Kavan was on his feet, bouncing on the bed, Fred and Ginger barking in time.

twenty

Humming, Elizabeth got ready for work, letting her thoughts and feelings of love for Kavan sink in and take hold. What an amazing feeling, she decided. Amazing.

Imagine, Jesus feels the same way about me, only more. She giggled.

Brushing her long eyelashes with black mascara, she paused and spoke to her reflection in the mirror. "You are in love, Elizabeth Lambert. You! Of all people."

The summer's events astounded her still—meeting Kavan and falling in love. Reuniting with the love of her Lord, knowing Jesus as her Friend. Realizing it was selfish pride not purpose driving her desire to go to grad school.

It seemed as if the Father had this special summer all wrapped up like a present, waiting for her. But she'd refused to accept it.

How gracious and kind He is to wait for me to surrender. Me and my foolish pride. I should write a book about it, she concluded, dabbing on her lipstick and leaving the bathroom.

In her room, she slipped on her black pumps and suit jacket before picking up the attaché case that contained her résumé.

At five minutes of eight, Elizabeth climbed behind the wheel of her car. She slipped the key into the ignition, then fished her cell phone from the attaché's side pocket. She pressed the number to autodial Will's office.

"This is Will Adams."

"Hi, it's Elizabeth. I'll be a few minutes late."

"No problem." He sounded distracted. Elizabeth pictured him intent on his computer, running production reports. "Anything I can do for you?" he asked.

"No, thanks."

She pressed the END button and tossed the phone into the passenger seat. Steering the VW north of town, Elizabeth felt exhilaration, coupled with nervous jitters.

Her life had turned upside down with the declaration of four simple words: Will you marry me? Yet somehow, the world finally seemed right, as if missing pieces were found and snapped into place.

At the next light, she turned left into Creager Electronics' blacktopped parking lot. Slipping the compact car into a visitor's slot, Elizabeth grabbed the leather attaché case and checked her appearance in the rearview mirror.

An austere receptionist greeted her at the front desk.

"I'd like to speak to someone in human resources."

"Do you have an appointment?" the woman asked.

"No, but I'd like to submit my résumé to the personnel manager."

The woman pursed her lips and clicked through the appointment calendar on her flat computer screen.

Lord, open a door for me, please, Elizabeth prayed. *I'm at Your mercy.*

"Have a seat." The woman motioned to a curved couch situated on the right side of the sleek receptionist desk.

"Thank you."

Elizabeth waited only a few minutes before a tall, lanky gentleman appeared through a set of brass-handled double doors. She rose and shook his extended hand.

"Brad Johnston, Director of Human Resources."

"Elizabeth Lambert. I'd like to submit my résumé." She flipped open the flap of her attaché and pulled out a linen sheet, her credentials listed in dark print.

"We aren't hiring, Miss Lambert." Brad Johnston accepted the paper.

Mustering her courage, she said, "Please review my résumé before deciding. You'll find I have all the qualifications."

He chuckled. "New grad?"

She nodded.

"I can tell. New grads always come to us reciting from the 'How to Interview' textbook."

Elizabeth met his brown gaze. "How else do you expect us to get companies like yours to consider us?"

"Touché," he said, grinning at her bravado. He skimmed her résumé. "MIT. Impressive. Graduated with a 4.0 average." His eyes shifted between her face and the paper in his hands. "Three terms in the artificial intelligence lab."

His fingers fidgeted with the paper, tapping it slightly. The rhythm matched the twittering beat of Elizabeth's heart. Brad Johnston puckered his lips in contemplation.

Surely he knows this is nerve-racking, Elizabeth thought.

After a second, he said, "Come with me. There are a few people I think would like to meet you."

At one fifteen, Elizabeth dashed through the doors of Lambert's Furniture and scurried up the stairs to her office. Tossing the attaché onto the floor by her desk, she slipped into her chair and booted up her computer.

"A few minutes late, huh?"

Elizabeth turned, startled. Will stood in her doorway, his arms folded across his broad chest. He glanced at his watch.

"Will, I'm sorry. Really. I didn't know it would take so long. Bad timing with all the end-of-the month figures due."

He chuckled. "By the light in your eyes and the smile on your face, it must be good."

Elizabeth sighed. "Yes, it's all good. God is so good. I can't believe it."

He nodded. "You'll tell me when you're ready, then."

"Yes, I promise. Thanks for understanding."

❧

At eleven o'clock Friday night, Kavan pulled up to the White Birch covered bridge. He cut the engine and reached for his flashlight. Stepping out of the truck, he saw a soft glow from the other side of the bridge, along the riverbank.

"Elizabeth?" he called, nerves causing his voice to pop and crack.

"Here," she answered.

The flashlight slipped in his perspiring palm as he fumbled with the light switch. "Hello." He stepped toward the sound of her voice. Thin ribbons of the half-moon's light filtered through the trees, dotting the path he walked.

Why did his mouth dry up like a desert in times like these? He tried to wet his dry lips with an even drier tongue. Kavan found Elizabeth perched on an old army blanket, the area lighted with several jar candles.

She patted the spot next to her.

"Hi." The golden glow of the candlelight fell on the soft curves of her face. Instinctively, he reached out and stroked the line along her jaw with his finger.

"Hi." She took his hand into hers and smiled.

Kavan's heart melted and pooled in his middle like warm syrup. "Elizabeth, you're. . ." He paused and drew a deep, shaky breath. With that came the sweet scent of her perfume. "You're killing me here. I don't know if my heart can take it."

She tenderly kissed the back of his hand. "I'm sorry, Kavan. I didn't mean to make this hard for you."

He settled next to her, wrapping his arms around his knees. Elizabeth leaned against him, and in that moment, it seemed as if all the pieces of his world came together. He kissed the top of her head. "I think I made this hard for myself, really. I knew you wanted to go to school."

"Me and my pride."

He lifted his arms to draw her into his embrace. She nestled her head against his shoulder, fitting perfectly there. "A woman has a right to her dreams."

"I judged girls who fell in love. I thought they were silly and stupid. Weak. I thought getting a bunch of degrees would declare me a success."

"Nothing wrong with a degree or two." He looked down at her, catching the image of a flickering flame in the blue hue of her eyes.

In one smooth motion, their faces drew close and their lips

touched, a kiss warm with love and emotion.

He cupped her face in his hand. "I really do love you."

"I know, and that totally ruined my life this summer."

"Glad to be of service."

She turned to face him. "Kavan, when you asked me to marry you, I realized for the first time in my life that I even wanted to be married. Hearing a man declare his love and desire to spend the rest of his life with me changed me. I tried to hang on to my ideals about grad school, but suddenly I couldn't remember them anymore. I prayed and prayed about it, and the Lord gave me His answer."

He couldn't help it. He reached up, pulled her face to his, and kissed her again. After that, he asked, "What did He say?"

"Lots of things," she teased.

Kavan slapped his hand over his heart and fell back against the blanket. "I'm dying here."

"I got a senior engineering position at Creager Electronics." She delivered the news without warning.

"What?" Kavan said, unsure of what he'd heard.

"I start at Creager Electronics in two weeks."

"What about grad school?"

She shook her head and shrugged. "Maybe someday. But the desire is gone. Creager's work in robotics is another interest of mine. Kavan, they offered me an amazing salary." She laughed. "At that point, all notions of grad school vanished."

He gaped at her for a long time, trying to gather his thoughts. "I'm stunned. I don't know what to say."

Elizabeth moved to her knees. "Kavan, I'm choosing love. Will you ask me again?"

He sat up like a shot. "Ask you to marry me?"

She nodded.

He knelt before her and took her hands into his. "Elizabeth, will you. . . No wait. First, let me say I love you. You are the Lord's answer to my heart's desire for a wife."

She trembled, a sob escaping her lips. "I love you, too."

Feeling a little giddy at the sound of those words, he leveled his rising emotions with a quick breath. He reached into his breast pocket and pulled out the blue velvet box. He popped open the top and lifted out the ring. Slipping the polished gold onto her ring finger, he asked once more, "Elizabeth, will you marry me?"

She gasped, catching the glitter of the ring in the candlelight. "Oh, Kavan, it's beautiful." She brushed her forehead with her other hand. "Wow, I never imagined. . ."

"That ring has a story you would not believe."

She looked from the ring to his face. "Really?"

"Really," he repeated. "Are you going to answer the question?"

She smiled. With metered, determined words, Elizabeth gave her answer, "Yes, Kavan Donovan, I will marry you."

Laughing, crying, shouting, they embraced and sealed their promise with a kiss.

"You've made me a very happy man."

"You've made me a very loved woman."

For the next hour, they sat under the stars talking and dreaming. Kavan amazed her with the story of the ring, spurring tears. The love and pleasure of the Lord astounded them.

At midnight, Kavan grabbed her hand and said, "Come with me."

"Where are we going?" she asked, laughing, jumping up.

"You'll see." Kavan led her to the bridge, walking under the high roof. He flashed his light along the beams, looking up, turning in a small circle.

"What are you looking for?"

"A spot." He grinned down at her. "Let's finalize this deal by carving our initials into the tapestry of White Birch's lovers."

Elizabeth found the spot. Next to her grandparents' initials, there was just enough space.

Kavan pulled out his pocketknife and carved *KD loves EL*.

"You know, it should say 'EL loves KD.' " She tiptoed up to kiss Kavan. " 'Cause EL truly does love KD."

"I suppose I should speak to your father."

"He'd like that," Elizabeth said.

"For now, how about telling Grandpa Matt and Grandma Betty?"

They woke Grandpa and Grandma to give them the good news. The older couple whooped and hollered like youngsters, hugging Elizabeth, then Kavan.

"Grandma," Grandpa said, doing a little jig around room, "we're having a wedding! Our Bethy is getting married."

A Letter To Our Readers

Dear Reader:

In order that we might better contribute to your reading enjoyment, we would appreciate your taking a few minutes to respond to the following questions. We welcome your comments and read each form and letter we receive. When completed, please return to the following:

Fiction Editor
Heartsong Presents
PO Box 719
Uhrichsville, Ohio 44683

1. Did you enjoy reading *Lambert's Pride* by Lynn A. Coleman and Rachel Hauck?
❏ Very much! I would like to see more books by this author!
❏ Moderately. I would have enjoyed it more if

_____
_____
_____

2. Are you a member of **Heartsong Presents**? ❏ Yes ❏ No
   If no, where did you purchase this book? _____
   _____

3. How would you rate, on a scale from 1 (poor) to 5 (superior), the cover design? _____

4. On a scale from 1 (poor) to 10 (superior), please rate the following elements.

____ Heroine   ____ Plot
____ Hero   ____ Inspirational theme
____ Setting   ____ Secondary characters

5. These characters were special because?_____
_____
_____

6. How has this book inspired your life?_____
_____
_____

7. What settings would you like to see covered in future
   Heartsong Presents books? _____
_____
_____

8. What are some inspirational themes you would like to see
   treated in future books? _____
_____
_____

9. Would you be interested in reading other **Heartsong
   Presents** titles? ❏ Yes   ❏ No

10. Please check your age range:
    ❏ Under 18   ❏ 18-24
    ❏ 25-34   ❏ 35-45
    ❏ 46-55   ❏ Over 55

Name_____
Occupation_____
Address_____
City_____ State_____ Zip_____

WISCONSIN

4 stories in 1

Can God truly touch tattered lives and heal hearts too heavy to hope? In the state of Wisconsin, four women encounter situations that seem unbearable—challenging their faith in God, in love, and in themselves. Can a broken marriage be renewed? Can God serve as the Husband for an unmarried woman, and as Father of her illegitimate child? Can two wounded spirits rebuild a faltering business—and their ruined lives? Can a lost love really be found again? Join popular author Andrea Boeshaar on a journey of discovery, as four women find a haven of hope.

Contemporary, paperback, 480 pages, 5 ³/₁₆"x 8"

♥ ♥ ♥ ♥ ♥ ♥ ♥ ♥ ❤ ♥ ♥ ♥ ♥ ♥ ♥ ♥ ♥

♥ ♥ ♥ ♥ ♥ ♥ ♥ ❤ ♥ ♥ ♥ ♥ ♥ ♥ ♥